the ultimate gift
exclusive movie edition

Rene Gutteridge

Based on the original novel by Jim Stovall

Published by
THOMAS NELSON™
Since 1798

ISBN-13: 978-0-7394-8246-9

foreword by Jim Stovall

Thank you for joining me on this truly incredible journey. In each person's life, there are a handful of amazing days. These are days that—from the vantage of an historical perspective—we can look back at over the years and realize that a single, solitary day inevitably changed our life forever. One of these amazing days for me occurred in late 1999.

Through a series of unintentional coincidences, I had become a motivational speaker for arena events around the world, and as a consequence of that, I became an author. I had written several how-to and biographical books drawing on my experience as a blind person and athlete, as well as founder and president of the Narrative Television Network. I had written a book about movie stars, athletes, and all manner of celebrities I had interviewed on television or worked with onstage. To make a long story a bit shorter, I had written everything I knew and a few things I only merely suspected.

When my publishers and readers continued to clamor for another book, I realized it was time for me to enter the realm of fiction. I had never written fiction before, but as with most other things in life, traveling uncharted waters didn't seem to bother me. I reasoned that if I had already written and published everything I knew, it was time to start making up things. Hence, on what I otherwise presumed was a normal day, I sat down to dictate what I assumed would be just another in a line of books.

My process in writing is different from any other author I have ever met. As a blind person myself, writing for me consists of dictating to a very competent lady in my office named Dorothy Thompson. I merely dictate the words as I wish them to appear in the book, and Dorothy takes responsibility for sentences, paragraphs, spelling, punctuation, and all related things that are a mystery to me.

I write very quickly, and I don't do edits or rewrites. People assume that my publishers have someone else to do the edits or rewrites, but in reality, with rare exceptions, the way I dictate my books to Dorothy is the way people around the world read them, word for word.

On that fateful day in 1999, I had nothing in my mind other than the first line of a story and the title, *The Ultimate Gift*. Over the next five days, a completed novel emerged, and I sent it off to my publisher, much as I had done with the previous five books. However, due to a corporate restructuring and eventual take-over at that publishing house, it was communicated to me that, although my publishers really liked *The Ultimate Gift,* they didn't want to release a novel. They were getting away from fiction. But since contracts had already been signed, I was informed that my publisher would put the book out into the marketplace . . . with no support. They simply were not willing to advertise or promote it.

Well, as I'm sure you can imagine, my little novel entitled *The Ultimate Gift* sat on bookshelves all across the country and simply died from lack of attention.

Then something happened that is still hard for me to believe; if I wrote it into one of my novels, no one else would believe it either. *The Ultimate Gift* started selling. But not in a normal way. I started getting calls from book distributors who were inquiring what I was doing to create these one hundred-, five hundred-, and even one thousand-book orders, as they had never before seen anything like that. Well, I simply didn't have a clue what I was doing to drive those orders, but I told the booksellers and distributors if they found out what was causing this to please let me know so we could continue doing it.

From that day to this, through a string of international publishers and without any major advertising or promotion at all, *The Ultimate Gift* has sold more than 3.5 million copies. Somehow, financial planners, brokers, insurance professionals, school teachers, university professors, clergy, and many others have been reading *The Ultimate Gift* and buying dozens and even hundreds of books to pass along to friends, clients, parishioners, and students. This is truly unprecedented.

As a blind person for the last two decades, one of my true joys in life has been discovering the National Library Service for the Blind. This agency makes special recorded books available to blind and visually impaired people across the country. Thanks to a high-speed tape player, I am able to consistently read a book each day. I am embarrassed to say when I had my eyesight and could read a book just as you are reading this one now, I don't know that I ever read an entire book cover to cover. But now, through my blindness, I have become not only a consistent and avid reader, but indeed a voracious reader.

Through all of those books throughout all of those years, occasionally there has been a title that impacted me so much I would recommend it to as many as four or five friends or colleagues. But when I learned that my very first effort at fiction, my little novel *The Ultimate Gift,* was being read and then passed along by all manner of individuals by the case lot and even the truckload, I was overwhelmed.

I had the added blessing, as I had included my phone number in *The Ultimate Gift,* of speaking literally to thousands of these avid readers and now disciples of the message. As these people have come to know, any time you have something to celebrate as part of your own *Ultimate Gift* journey or if you're in one of those periods when *The Ultimate Gift* magic and message doesn't seem to apply to your current dilemma, I am as close as the nearest telephone at 918-627-1000. To this day, people continue to call for more books and speeches and information about the movie and sequel books, including *The Ultimate Life*. I sit here each and every day thankful that providence put me in the right place at the right time on that amazing day in 1999.

As *The Ultimate Gift* continued to skyrocket as a cultural icon, I was contacted by several major movie studios regarding making *The Ultimate Gift* into a movie. As owner and CEO of a television network, I have worked in and around the movie and entertainment industry for a number of years and know at least one of the pitfalls; therefore, each time a studio presented me with a contract to make *The Ultimate Gift* into a movie, I inserted a clause into the contract that stated I would have to approve the movie script. After several frustrating experiences, I had resigned myself to the probability that *The Ultimate Gift* would never be a movie because no one was committed to keeping the magic and the message intact.

Then came the day when Rick Eldridge called me, and from that initial conversation and Rick's commitment to the message, *The Ultimate Gift* movie was born. Rick became my partner and my friend, and a creative force in propelling *The Ultimate Gift* movie and movement ahead. As producer of *The Ultimate Gift* movie, Rick Eldridge not only allowed me but encouraged me to maintain script approval and to provide input into casting, music, and every element of the film. He even allowed me to play a brief part in the movie. When you're watching *The Ultimate Gift* on the big screen, near the end of the film there is a brief scene involving a limo driver delivering a few lines. That would be me. I find it ironic and a bit comical that somehow the blind guy got to be the limo driver—or at least I can say I play one in the movies.

The Ultimate Gift movie and this novelization of it repackage and share a vital piece of the message, fully presented in the original *The Ultimate Gift* novel. I believe that books can change people's minds and ideas and, therefore, their lives, as continues to happen with *The Ultimate Gift* novel. But movies can change a culture. Therefore, together we can *Share the Gift* and *Change the World.*

Jim Stovall
2007
Jim@JimStovall.com

chapter 1

Charlotte, North Carolina
Present Day

Sir . . . he's gone."

Theophilus Hamilton stood near the large glass window that framed a world he hardly understood anymore. He didn't turn around but instead let his gaze fall to the busy city below. A deep sadness tangled his words, so he took a moment to compose himself. The inevitable had finally come, but it didn't make it any easier.

He stayed at the window as he addressed Miss Hastings. "Contact family members, the various corporate boards and business interests . . ." He sighed. There was a lot to take care of. Now wasn't the time to mourn. And Hamilton knew that perhaps he mourned more for what Red had endured in life. Red was at peace now, but there would be nothing resembling peace in the wake of his death. "And let's call a meeting."

"Yes, sir," Miss Hastings said. She turned to leave the room, then stopped and turned back to Hamilton. "Sir, I am so sorry for your loss." She pulled the heavy oak doors of his office closed.

Clutching his cane, he gazed out the dark window and wondered how well he would be able to tolerate the wolves that had been waiting and circling for days now. Oh, yes, they would put on their sad faces. Some of them. Others would adopt a false solicitousness. No matter. Everything was set into motion now; no man could change it. And he doubted it would change any man, either.

But for a man whose life had gone terribly wrong in so many different ways, he'd had hope all the way to the end.

Hamilton closed his eyes. The older he got, the less he held out much optimism for anything. But maybe, just maybe, he had a little, too.

His mind wandered back to the first time he'd ever heard Red's voice. It had been a phone call, placed to Hamilton right after he'd graduated from law school.

"Am I speaking with Theophilus Hamilton?"

"Sir, yes—Yes, sir. This is he."

"Name's Howard Stevens. You can call me Red. I need a lawyer for a few business ideas I have, a few still in the dream stage."

Hamilton smiled now. Red Stevens and his dreams. He was at peace. But Theophilus understood peace would not be a part of his own immediate future.

◇ ◇ ◇

The day couldn't have been grayer. Hamilton stood near the pastor, surveying the five-hundred-plus mourners who clustered around the shiny mahogany casket of Red Stevens. Flowers, bright and white, were the only color among a graveyard filled with stately, aboveground tombs and important people all dressed in suitable dark clothing, every single one carrying a black umbrella. Their faces reflected more aversion to the rain they were forced to stand in than to the death of the man they were here to lament.

Behind the mourners and down the hill a little, Hamilton spotted one pink umbrella, which was doing a poor job of protecting its keeper from the rain, since the young girl wasn't putting it over her head. Instead, she seemed to be the only one embracing the moment, with her face tilted upward to the sky as it bathed her in wetness.

Hamilton sighed. Oh, how he wished there could be more of that kind of goodness and innocence in the world.

The pastor, hunched under his own black umbrella, cupping his little black book, was doing his best to uphold the sanctity of the moment. "Though the skies may weep," he said, "the Bible assures us that 'precious in the sight of the Lord is the death of his saints.'"

No one—near Hamilton, anyway—looked as though they cared at all what the Bible said. Red's two sons, Bill and Jack, stood just three feet away, oblivious to the idea they were supposed to appear sorrowful.

"I wonder who the old man negotiated with for the rain," Jack said with a cynical smile to Bill, Red's oldest.

"Well, it's a sure bet he's laughing, watching us get soaked."

"Yeah, well, now it's his turn," Jack said.

"There's not a person here," the pastor continued, "whose life in some way has not been touched by Howard 'Red' Stevens."

Hamilton watched Jack and Bill glance at each other and roll their eyes. Jack, the playboy of the family, pulled up the sleeve of his coat and looked at his watch. Bill glanced down at some sort of organizing device or cell phone in his hand, then quietly put it back in his pocket. It was all Hamilton could do not to say something, but that wasn't his way. And it hadn't been Red's either. He'd let his children become what they'd become. He'd tried a time or two to step in and talk some sense into any of them who would listen, but they never listened unless he was talking in the language of dollar signs.

Hamilton's gaze found its way back to the little girl, who seemed intent on getting wet. He wondered why such a young girl felt the need to wear such dark lipstick. She couldn't have been more than ten years old, but her lips were stained the color of wine grapes. What was the world coming to? But he smiled as the mother suddenly noticed the umbrella to her side and rushed to put it back in its place, much to the young girl's disappointment.

"Red often quoted Malcolm Muggeridge," the pastor said to a crowd growing more agitated with every wet minute that went by, "saying that 'every happening, great or small, is a parable by which God speaks to us; and the art of life is to get the message.'

May the message of Red Stevens continue in the hearts of those he leaves behind."

The pastor seemed to sense he was losing their interest. He turned to Bill. "Bill?" He gestured toward the casket.

"Uh . . . yes," Bill said, stepping forward. Reaching into his coat, he pulled out a small canister. "Even though Dad moved his corporate offices from Texas many years ago, for tax reasons, he always said he wanted to be buried under Texas soil." He opened the canister and shook some dirt onto the casket, then stepped back.

Somebody touched Hamilton's elbow. He didn't have to turn around. He knew it was Miss Hastings, assuring him he was right for keeping silent and avoiding a scene.

Suddenly the loud rumblings of a car caused the entire crowd to turn as a vintage 1971 Dodge Charger R/T slowed on the small cemetery road below. What little dirt was left on the casket fell off as the ground shook from the revving engine. Hamilton could hardly stop himself from throwing up his hands in disgust. But then again, neither could the other mourners, whose mouths hung open at the sight of the yellow-and-black muscle car roaring to a stop in front of them.

The young man getting out of the car was apparently the only one who hadn't gotten the family memo about what kind of etiquette was expected. He flung the car door open, nursing a cigarette and likely a bad hangover, judging by the state of his clothes and hair. Some hideous rock-and-roll song thumped against the backdrop of the rainstorm, until he turned it off and rose out of the car. He wore black sunglasses and an expression that might've been worse if they could see his eyes. Beside him an expressionless young woman appeared in a taut black dress that spoke to the idea she might be at the wrong social event.

"Is that him?" Miss Hastings whispered.

"That's him." Hamilton sighed. He watched Jason Stevens walk up the small hill, dismissing his cigarette as he tossed it aside into a puddle. He also dismissed his girlfriend and two others who had crawled unsteadily from the backseat of the car, walking ahead of all of them and heading straight for his mother, Sarah.

"Mom," he said.

Even with all the Botox she'd managed over the years, his mother was able to lift her eyebrows high in a frightful expression of embarrassment and shock. "You're late!" she said in a sharp tone.

Jason Stevens propped his sunglasses on top of his head, glancing around at his family members with the kind of attitude that got you cut out of the will.

Then he offered a perfectly inappropriate smile. "For what?"

chapter 2

Hamilton was glad they'd called the meeting for earlier rather than later. He'd been dreading this since he rose out of bed, and it was time to get it over with. From his office, he could hear them all talking over each other. You'd never know they were a family, apart from a DNA test. And in a few cases, even that likely wouldn't be relevant.

Miss Hastings waited patiently at his door, her fingers intertwined, her face expectant. A small smile emerged as she watched him leave the safety of his desk.

He gave her a knowing glance. "Let's get this over with."

"Yes, sir."

"Everything is in order? I don't want to have to be in there any longer than necessary."

"We're ready for you, sir."

Hamilton, followed closely by Miss Hastings, shuffled to the conference room with the aid of a cane. As big as it was, the room suddenly seemed small. A horde of people had taken it over, huddling in groups. Every family member, save one, was there, along with their various entourages. As Hamilton walked in, greedy faces turned to him. The room hushed, but in their eyes Hamilton could see anxious, animal-like hunger for what awaited them. Some licked their lips. Others suppressed eager smiles. And all of their lawyers held suspicious expressions.

"Good morning," Hamilton said, glancing at each of them in turn. "Before we start, I'd like to say how much Red meant to me personally. As you know, we started out as business partners and we ended up as friends. I am deeply grieved by his passing."

"Yes, well, that's very nice," Bill said. "Now, may we proceed?"

They wanted business? Fine. Business it would be. Hamilton kept his expression even and his tone professional as he pulled out his chair and sat between his two associates, Gregory and Linda.

"Red's will is in his own words," Hamilton began. "Still, every bit is legal and binding—"

"Blah, blah, blah," a teenager said from the corner of the room.

"And so," Hamilton continued, looking down at the document in front of him. He put on his reading glasses. "'My eldest son, Bill, I leave my company, Panhandle Oil and Gas . . .'"

"Currently worth six hundred million dollars," Gregory stated as he looked at the laptop in front of him.

Hamilton glanced up to see Bill smiling at his attorney. "'However,'" Hamilton continued to read, "'Bill, since you had zero interest in my company while I was alive, I don't imagine that will change much after my death. Therefore, the board will maintain control.'"

One of Bill's lawyers actually gasped. "Excuse me," he said, as if he had some authority in the matter, "but my client would like to explore all of his options—"

"Your client has no more options," Hamilton said bluntly. He watched anger simmer beneath Bill's cold stare and offered a polite and mannerly smile in return.

Bill was about to retort when Linda said, "One of those instructions Mr. Hamilton skipped over is Red's desire that each of you vacate after receiving your portion of the estate."

Bill stood there wide eyed, seemingly unable to understand it was his time to "vacate." His lawyer looked as if he might faint.

"As in leave the room," Linda added.

Bill looked angrily at his attorney. "She can't talk to me like that. Do something!"

Hamilton was already tired of this, and it was just round one. "You can go now, Mr. Stevens."

"What?" Bill exclaimed. His lawyer whispered something in his ear, which didn't appear to lower Bill's frustration, but he grabbed his briefcase. "All right. Fine. Fine!"

His other lawyer quickly gathered the wife and kids, herding them out the door. All the way into the elevator they could be heard bickering. "I have *never* been so humiliated! And did you see that old man talk to me that way? And you guys sat there and said absolutely nothing!"

Hamilton patiently waited for the elevator doors to close before proceeding. He turned to page two and looked up at Ruth, Red Stevens's only daughter. There was a bit of terror in her overdone eyes. "Next . . ."

○ ○ ○

Jason Stevens heard shouting in the elevator shafts. The doors slid open on the eighth floor, and he walked out. Yes, it was Bill's voice, heard as it plunged downward in another elevator. There were other voices coming from the boardroom, and he stood for a moment and listened. The last thing he wanted was to be in there. Noticing a nice leather chair in the small waiting room outside, he hopped over its back and fell into it sideways, swinging his knees over the armrest. He grabbed a nearby magazine, just for the effect, but he was all ears as he heard his aunt's screechy voice floating out.

"That's it?" she asked. "A cow farm?"

Jason smiled. Oh, this was going to be fun. In a spinal-tap sort of way.

Someone explained, "A ten-thousand-acre cow farm."

Suddenly Ruth was at the door, her husband, Rick, in tow. She didn't even notice Jason as she steamed past. "Well, what's that worth, anyway?"

Rick hurried behind her like a needy animal. "Ruth, come on.

Come here. What exactly do we get?"

"A place for you to take your mistress," Ruth spat. Jason lowered his magazine just in time to see her slam her hand against the elevator button. *Moo.* Let the insanity begin.

"I want to see everything! Full disclosure!" That was Jack. He had by far the loudest voice and the most scandalous secrets, and he was always the first one to get drunk at a party.

"Good day, Mr. Stevens," another voice replied.

Suddenly Jack was out in the hallway with his lawyer. Again, nobody noticed Jason as he observed like a fly on the wall.

"This is a long way from over, Jack," the lawyer was saying, trying to guide him toward the elevator.

"You said it was a slam dunk!"

"Jack, I'll handle it."

Jack shoved his way past the lawyer, yelling at his wife and kids to hurry up. They hustled toward him and all got on the elevator together. No one said a word.

"'To Sarah, the widow of my late son Jay Howard Stevens . . .'"

Jason suddenly felt sick in the pit of his stomach. He was going to have to deal with his mother. Why had he even showed up? He'd told her he wasn't coming, but he'd come anyway. He hated that, but she could heap a lot of guilt on, and sometimes it was worth just doing what she wanted.

"'. . . I am truly sorry for the events of the past. Please know that Jay's death represents the greatest tragedy I have ever experienced . . .'"

Anger replaced whatever emotion lingered in the depths of

his stomach. What a crock. How could his mother stand to hear it?

"'. . . I leave you control of my Myer's Park estate where you now reside and a managed trust for expenses as long as you live. Since your choice of male companionship is vast and varied, the deed and title for the house will remain under the control of my trustees.'"

"Good day, Mr. Hamilton," he heard his mother say, and then she was out the door. She was the only one to notice him there, and she stomped over, slapping his feet down off the chair. Behind her was one of her boyfriends, clinging to her like static and looking remarkably younger than the last time Jason had seen him.

Inside the boardroom, he heard a woman say, "It's amazing just how far the fruit can fall from the tree."

"And still roll a great distance," came Hamilton's reply.

His mother glared at him as they made their way to the elevators. "Nice of you to show up. You're in time for nothin'. Let's go."

Jason was just stepping into the elevator, trying to remember the name of his mother's latest boyfriend, when he heard his name called.

He paused, then stepped back out of the elevator. He heard it again.

"Jason?"

Through the open door, he studied the man still sitting in the boardroom—an older, distinguished-looking black gentleman with gray at the temples, hunched shoulders, and disappointment in his tired-looking eyes. "How do you know my name?" Jason asked.

"It's my business to know everyone named in your grand-father's will."

Jason glanced at his mother, then back at this man. "Well, let's cut the BS, 'cause I know what he left me. Nothing."

"Walk away," the man said, "and you'll never know, will you?"

He could hear his mother's sigh fill the elevator. Against his better judgment he let go of the elevator door. It swished closed as he walked toward the conference room, where two associates were just leaving. As he entered, they returned with a sealed box he guessed was supposed to look impressive.

"So what's in the box?" he asked Hamilton.

"Your inheritance. Have a seat." It was a command, not a request.

Jason fell into the chair with a sloppy indifference. Terrific. How ludicrous could this get? What was next? A map to some buried pirate treasure? He knew it: Red was a pirate.

"I am Mr. Hamilton. This is Miss Hastings."

Jason glanced at the woman, who had an air of avid politeness about her.

Hamilton gestured toward the box. "Does the box or the seal appear to have been tampered with in any way?"

Jason shrugged. "No."

"Then," said Hamilton with a ridiculous amount of serious-ness, "therefore witness this day that I am breaking the seal affixed in my presence by Red himself. Miss Hastings?" He reached into the box and pulled out a DVD, which he handed to Miss Hastings.

"Yes, sir."

Jason watched Miss Hastings walk to the back of the room. Suddenly the conference room went dark, and before him a panel slid up, revealing a screen. A video image of his grandfather appeared.

"Are we on?" his grandfather asked.

A voice off screen said he was.

Jason watched as his grandfather stared into the camera with steely eyes and a tightly drawn mouth. There was still that part of him that was a cowboy, Jason observed. Maybe he should've stuck to his ranch and left everyone else alone. Things would've been better that way. But then again, Red had never cared much about what affected who or why.

"Well, then," he continued, "if you're watching this, I must be dead. That's a strange concept. How was my funeral? Well attended? Hope it rained."

Jason rolled his eyes and kicked his feet up on the table. That was a joke Red used to tell. Something about it raining at his funeral. Jason couldn't remember it, but whatever it was, it was stupid.

He felt Hamilton's hand on his feet, pushing them off the table.

"Hamilton? Miss Hastings? Hope you're having a better day than I am. But if you've just been with my family, I doubt it."

Jason glanced at Hamilton, who chuckled with Miss Hastings at the joke.

"Jason," Red continued, "I made a lot of mistakes with our family. But you're the one I think I hurt the most."

Jason suddenly felt strangely vulnerable. Here he was sitting in a dark room with strangers, and his grandfather felt the need to confess some things to him? He'd had plenty of time in life to do it. The coward had left it on a tape? Hardly noble. And, Jason guessed, not particularly sincere either.

"The only way I can make it up to you is to not give you anything."

"I knew it." Jason stood. It was time to go. He didn't need this.

"What I mean by that is I'm not giving you anything *just yet*. So sit back down there."

Jason glanced at Hamilton, embarrassment running through him at the fact he was so predictable. He slowly sat back down. Yeah, fine. The old man had known Jason would stand. So what? There was a whole lot more he didn't know.

Red continued. "I've been thinking about this for a long time. How can I give you something and not have it ruin you like your uncles and aunts? Even some of their kids. So I want to give you a gift. A series of gifts leading up to . . . Well, I'm gonna call it the ultimate gift." Red gestured like that was significant. Then his tone grew serious. "Now, you fail in any way, it's over. You get nothing. And everything you do must be to Mr. Hamilton's satisfaction."

Jason exchanged a glance with Hamilton, who didn't seem the least bit stirred by anything they were hearing. Instead, his eyes were stern, leaving the rest of his face expressionless.

"You might want to make friends with him sooner than later," Red said with a small smile. Then the video faded to black and the lights came back on.

Jason tried to process everything, but before he could, Miss Hastings was by his side, handing him an electronic device. "This is a voice-activated Conversay," she said. "It allows two-way communication between our office and you, and you can also replay Red's messages on it if you need to."

Jason tried several times to think of something to say, but nothing was coming out.

An assistant entered the room and handed Hamilton a sheet of paper. Scanning it, he nodded satisfactorily. "Ah, good. There's a flight to Houston tomorrow at seven a.m.," he told Jason.

"As in morning? Seven a.m.?"

"Yes, *that* seven a.m."

"For what?"

"You have until then to accept."

Jason looked anxiously at them. "Why do I have to go?"

"You'll find out when you get there," Hamilton said with a take-it-or-leave-it tone.

Jason headed for the door. "This is whacked."

"You might want to rethink that," Hamilton said.

Jason stopped and turned. He was tired of being bullied by this man and his mysterious box. "What could he possibly give me that he hasn't already taken away? Huh? He can go to hell. Both of you can go to hell."

○ ○ ○

Noise. Lots of it. And that's the way Jason liked it. Louder, bigger, faster, higher. People swarmed from one room to another, dancing, talking, drinking. He set his glass down and walked away from it all.

He found himself alone in a bedroom, staring at a picture frame. His father smiled back, standing beside a young boy Jason hardly recognized anymore. He was looking more like his father and less like the boy he used to be. Even his hair, cut short, had darkened with age. A plaque on the frame read "Boys Night Out."

"Hi."

Caitlin. Jason turned. "Hi."

She smiled, then gazed toward the party. "Why are you in here?"

"No reason."

"How was your day?"

"I'm not sure." Jason decided to walk the crowd.

"What do you mean?" Caitlin asked, following him.

"My grandfather may have left me something."

Caitlin's eyes widened, sparkling in the glow of the mood lighting. "Yeah?"

"I'm just trying to figure it out."

"You mean it's not cash?"

"I don't know."

"You don't know?"

Jason turned from her. Yeah, it was as complicated as it sounded.

More complicated. He picked up the glass he'd set down and finished it off with his back to her. "Well, if I want to play into his little power trip, I gotta go pick it up."

"Where?"

Jason could hardly bring himself to say it. He didn't want this to own him. Nothing had ever owned him before. "Texas."

"Eck." Caitlin looked repulsed.

"You know what? I'm not going."

A flirtatious smile curved over her glossy lips. "Well, aren't you at least curious?" she said, trying to keep up with him as he made his way to the balcony. "What if it's gold?"

"He ruined my life. My best revenge is to just ignore him. Besides, I've got a trust fund. Worst-case scenario, I'll live off my mom." That *was* the worst-case scenario, beyond being tortured or made to drive anything with six cylinders. He looked at Caitlin. "I don't need his money."

"Yeah, but one can always use some extra walking-around money."

"Not if I have to sell my soul."

Laughter erupted from inside the penthouse. The partygoers were oblivious to how obnoxious his life had just become.

Caitlin looked to be in serious thought. "But if you had to," she said, "at least try to get as much out of him as you can. I mean, my gosh, what if you actually had to get a job sometime?"

Jason sighed. *Then* he'd sell his soul, but not a second before.

chapter 3

There was nothing better than riding a motorcycle into a tunnel or some sort of covered parking. Jason revved his engine, and those people near the curb hurried toward the door, giving him disgusted looks. He slowed his V-Max down and pulled to the curb, stopping right at the "Do Not Park" sign and resting the bike on its kickstand. As he hopped off and headed for the automatic doors, he glanced back and laughed. Already a police officer had pulled his pad out and was writing a ticket.

Standing just inside the terminal doors was Miss Hastings. Jason liked her. Wished his mom had been that kind of woman. There was no denying the skepticism, and a bit of irritation, in her eyes. But she seemed to be the only one who didn't look down on him. He walked straight up to her and grabbed the Conversay and the plane ticket she held out to him. When she looked meaningfully at the motorcycle outside, he grinned.

"Police escort . . . sort of." He strolled toward the security gate.

But the fun soon ended when he was asked to remove his shoes and succumb to search by magic wand. He hated flying commercial. What was Red trying to prove? Why would he go to all this trouble for a grandson he hardly knew anymore? It seemed ridiculous. Why not just give all his money to Bill Gates and be done with it? Warren Buffet had. It had been all the talk for a while—the second-richest man in the world giving the first-richest man all his money. It was absurd and genius all at once. Especially if you wanted to alienate your family.

Which Red had done in textbook form. Red's children had tolerated him, but everyone knew it was only because they didn't want to be cut out of the will. Jason himself hadn't been able to stand Red.

So what was all this about? The old man making up for what he'd done? Impossible. But Jason had to admit he was curious. Maybe that's why he'd come today. And to wipe that smug look off Hamilton's face.

He arrived at the gate just in time to board. Swinging his bag over his shoulder, he walked onto the plane and spotted an empty seat in first class. Without hesitation, he threw his bag down and fell into the plush leather. Soon enough they'd hit thirty thousand feet, and thanks to a drink or two he'd be out like a baby.

"Uh, excuse me, sir."

Jason looked up to find the stern face of a male flight attendant above him.

"Um, can I . . . can I see your boarding pass again?"

Jason sighed. Obviously nothing was going to be easy. He pulled it out of his pocket and handed it to him.

The attendant looked it over and turned it toward him. "Thank you. Yeah, see, this is, um . . . I'm sorry, this is for coach."

"That's impossible."

"No. It's, uh, 32B."

"Well, change it."

"You can't do that, sir. We can't change it. It's a Q fare." The attendant cleared his throat. "You can't, um, upgrade."

Jason glared at him. "Do you have any idea who I am?"

The attendant's eyes narrowed a bit. "I know exactly who you are. You're the guy in seat 32B. Here we go." He stepped back a little and gestured toward the back of the plane like he was pointing to an emergency exit.

"Whatever." Jason grabbed his bag and stomped toward the back of the plane. Then he saw where he was supposed to sit. "You have got to be kidding me!"

Heads snapped up as everyone's attention focused on him. But Jason's attention was on the snoring man next to the window and the timid-looking mother who was bouncing a screaming four-month-old on her lap. He watched trepidation wash over the mother as she looked up at him. It couldn't have been more than the sense of dread that was filling him by the second.

21

"Sorry," she said, unbuckling her seatbelt and standing so he could slide in.

Shoving his bag under the seat in front of him, he snapped his seatbelt and folded his arms together. The guy next to him looked like his head could fall on Jason's shoulder at any minute. The mother glanced at him apologetically. "It could be worse," she said, smiling.

"Really." Jason couldn't imagine how.

And then, through the thin wall behind him, he heard the toilet flush.

○ ○ ○

It was official. He was never going to have kids. The baby hadn't stopped crying from the time they took off until they landed. That is, until the flight attendant announced they could deboard. Then the baby fell asleep and the mother begged Jason not to make any loud noises or move quickly. To top it all off, the flight attendant had had the nerve to ask Jason if he would mind carrying the diaper bag out for the woman.

Rid of that responsibility, he now had to figure out what he was supposed to do. He looked around in baggage claim for someone holding a sign with his name on it, but nobody seemed to be looking for him.

"Great." He walked outside and stood on the curb, pulling out the Conversay and pushing the green button.

After a few seconds, Miss Hastings's face filled the small screen.

"Hello, Jason."

"So what is this? One of those things my Aunt Martha had to wear or what?"

"I see you're at the Houston airport." She seemed to be looking at something else on her computer screen. "Baggage claim."

Jason's attention was diverted by an older man circling him like a hawk. Jason watched him take a long look at him. "You got a problem?"

"You don't look like you worked a day in your life," the man said.

"Great. The Amazing Kreskin." Jason turned back to the image of Miss Hastings. "Look, I don't know what I'm supposed to be doing because no one's been able—"

The man who'd been staring him down grabbed his bag and threw it into the back of his silver double-cab pickup.

"Hey!" Jason shouted.

"I'm Gus. I'm your ride. Get in."

Jason looked at Miss Hastings's tiny face on the screen. "Never mind." Turning off the Conversay, he grabbed the truck's door handle and hopped in. With a brief look, Gus pulled from the curb before Jason had even had a chance to shut the door.

"Easy, cowboy," Jason said, settling into his seat.

Gus, it seemed, was a man of few words. With one hand draped over the steering wheel like the truck might not need to turn for the next several days, he chewed on something Jason couldn't identify. Every once in a while, he would look sideways at Jason, almost as if he'd forgotten he was there.

Jason wished he could forget too. But before he knew it, he had finally fallen asleep to a Patsy Cline tune.

◇ ◇ ◇

Jason's eyes slowly opened, but everything was blurry. Was he hung over again? He tried to sit up, but a crick in his neck had him cringing. He noticed his head was against the window of a . . . truck. He groaned. Oh, yeah. Gus.

Sitting up a little, he gazed out the window at . . . nothing. Flat, green fields were surrounded by lines of endless fences. It was official. Texas was hell.

Gus looked over at Jason. "Sorry about your grandfather's passing. We go way back."

Good for you.

"He was some man. Loved to work." Gus chuckled. "The man just loved hard work."

"Right. Mind if I smoke?"

"It's a free country."

Could've fooled me. Jason felt in the front pocket of his jacket, then checked his jean pockets. He tried to restrain from cursing. That's all he needed, to be in need of a nicotine fix.

He tried a polite voice. "Can you stop at the next convenience store?"

"Convenience store?"

"Please." Nicotine could make him awfully desperate.

Gus's eyes stayed on the road. "Well, the last store's about fifty miles back. We've been on my property for the last thirty minutes or so." He glanced sideways and smiled at what must've been a very shocked expression on Jason's face. Okay, so this guy owned a good portion of hell. Things were getting better by the second. And without nicotine.

Ten more minutes passed before Gus turned down a modest road. At the end was an enormous farmhouse nestled between trees and some hills, which broke the view to what was sure to be thousands more monotonous acres. A wide but tidy porch hugged the front of the house, complete with rocking chairs. *Martha Stewart, here we come.*

As Jason closed the truck door, Gus made his way around to him. "Seein' as how you're Red's grandson, you'll stay in the main house with us. I know it ain't much, but the little lady just wanted a modest place."

Jason's glance slid toward the house. Maybe in comparison to what they'd just driven through, this was considered modest.

"Dinner's in an hour, breakfast at five." Gus started toward the front door of his home.

"Uh . . . Gus? Aren't you forgetting something?" Jason tried his best smile through the headache that was coming on.

"I don't think so. Shoot."

"The gift?" A miracle would be if it included a pack of cigarettes.

Gus broke into laughter, holding his belly and shaking his head, then disappeared inside the house.

If this was hell, then Gus was the devil, and the devil apparently liked his breakfast before the sun rose.

◇ ◇ ◇

Gus owned one television, and he'd parked himself in front of it right after dinner, then dozed off, sleeping through a series of window-rattling snores Jason could hear all the way up the stairs. Who could blame him? Patsy Cline could put anybody to sleep. But Jason didn't dare sneak downstairs to turn it off. There was no telling what kind of crazy that would bring out in Gus.

Falling onto his bed, Jason kicked his shoes off and stared at the work clothes—including boots, gloves, pants, and a flannel shirt—apparently laid out for him. It didn't bode well for the future. He rolled to his back and pulled out his cell phone. Still no signal. It was a wonder they had running water and electricity out here.

Cradling his phone, he got comfortable. Why not? He was stuck here indefinitely. This was his grandfather's idea of fun—to send his grandson on some stupid trip to the far country. Jason shook his head at the thought. It angered him. Why couldn't the old man just die and be done with it? Why did he have to keep reminding everyone who he was and what he could do?

Jason was very aware of what he could do.

He closed his eyes, and though he didn't want to, he knew he would dream about his dad.

chapter 4

gus stared at the empty seat at the breakfast table, watching the stairs for any sign of movement. The only noise was his own fork scooping the eggs off his plate.

That boy was going to be awfully hungry.

He finished his coffee and climbed the stairs, each heavy step of his work boot making enough noise to rouse the farm animals. Outside Jason's room, he turned the doorknob and flung it open, kind of hoping to catch the kid asleep.

Gus smiled.

Walking over to the side of the bed, he nudged the kid on the shoulder. Dead to the world.

"Hey. City boy. Breakfast is over."

At the word *breakfast,* Jason moved a little. Gus sighed. He didn't have the patience for this. He couldn't even remember the last time he'd actually had to wake someone up in the morning.

"Don't you have some kind of gizmo to wake you up?" Gus eyed the phone Jason had been carrying with him everywhere he went, then grabbed the boy's shoulder, shaking him enough to get his eyes to open.

The kid moaned and mumbled, "Beat it."

Beat it? Gus turned and stomped out of the room, muttering to himself as he marched down the stairs and out the back door. What kind of crazy was this kid? And what had Red gotten him into now? Red always had liked to take on the impossible.

Opening the barn door, Gus turned on the lantern. He held the lamp up and looked around until he spotted what he was looking for. "There you are," he said through an ornery grin. Grabbing it, he walked back into the house and went up the stairs, making more noise than a cowbell.

But still Jason slept, the blanket tangled around his legs and an arm falling over the side. *Good grief. Pigs have more ambition than this kid,* Gus thought. *At least they get up to eat.*

Firing up the cattle prod, he touched it to Jason's backside.

"Augh!" Jolted by the electric shock, Jason let out a yelp. "What is your problem?"

"Mornin'!"

○ ◇ ○

It took another fifteen minutes for the kid to get ready. How hard was it to put on work clothes? He was probably up there styling his hair and putting on cologne.

Gus waited below, eyeing the clock. He was about ready to go up and drag the kid downstairs in his underwear if he had to, but then Jason emerged, slowly lifting one foot in front of the other like his boots were made of concrete. Descending at that rate, he might be lucky to finish by midnight.

Without a word, Gus headed through the dining room with Jason trailing him. The kid looked around as the kitchen staff cleared the dishes and leftovers.

"Time to get to work. Sun'll be up soon. Let's go!" Gus hollered.

Jason lurched for a plate, snagging a piece of bacon and dry toast and trying to shovel the food into his mouth as fast as possible. Gus headed for the door.

Outside, he opened the truck door and held it as Jason stumbled from the house and climbed in. Then, hopping into the driver's seat, he stared at the kid. "Breakfast is at five. If you want breakfast, get yourself up and dressed, then come down. We don't come down in our pajamas. Washed, dressed, and then you eat. That's the way it is."

He did feel a little sorry for the kid. He looked like he might be living in his own personal nightmare. Gus chuckled. And the day had yet to begin.

As they drove along, Gus let the morning breeze do most of the talking. He liked this time of day, when the sun came over the horizon, when the air was still cool and crisp, the shadows of

29

the night diminishing into the soft hazy dew. Everything smelled fresh and new. He studied the pastures, counted the cattle by the fences, and wondered what was going through Jason Stevens's mind.

"Your granddad and I started out together wildcattin' oil wells down in Louisiana," he said, just as Jason looked like he might be drifting off to sleep again. "Made some money and we each bought cattle spreads as a hedge against the oil runnin' out."

Jason feigned interest.

"Of course, you ain't really made it unless you own your own little piece of Texas, right?"

"Right."

Gus pulled the truck to the side of the road and got out. Jason was barely out of the truck by the time Gus had unloaded his post-hole digger. Walking down the ditch and up the other side, Gus first lined up the string for the rest of the fence. Then he plunged the digger into the earth. Grabbing the dirt, he pulled it out and dropped it beside the hole. Eight more times and the hole was deep enough. Gus wiped the sweat already beading his brow, picked up a post, and dropped it in. Shoveling the dirt around the hole, he used his feet to pack it around the base until the post was secure.

Standing, he looked at Jason, taking a moment to catch his breath. "Just from there. Eight feet from the center."

"What?"

"Lunch'll be sent round about eleven," Gus said, walking to his truck. He watched the kid look down the fence line.

"Well, how far am I supposed to go?"

Gus smiled. "Don't worry. You'll run out of posts before you run out of Texas."

Jason went a little pale.

"Wish I had a dollar for every fence post I ever set." Gus looked down the fence line, then back at Jason. "Matter of fact, I do."

◊ ◊ ◊

The dust cloud from Gus's departure was all that was left. Jason looked in every direction, but he seemed to be the only living thing around. He couldn't even see the cattle. Where were all those animals Gus had been bragging about?

Plopping himself down on top of the stack of wooden posts, Jason thought for a brief moment he might luck out and get a cell phone signal. But no.

He pulled out the Conversay, stared at it, and put it back in his pocket. That was all he needed . . . Hamilton breathing down his neck.

He sat back and was getting comfortable on the stack when he noticed the sunrise. He wasn't sure he'd ever seen a sunrise in real life. Bright orange and purple streaks cut into the blue sky that was emerging. The morning breeze tickled his face. He took in a deep breath. Despite the phantom cattle, it actually smelled good out here.

Reclining, with his arms stretched out on either side, Jason laid his head back. Perfect napping environment.

○ ○ ○

It was like the day had repeated itself all over again. There he stood, out in the middle of nowhere as the roar of Gus's truck faded, staring at the pile of wood and wire. And up the sun came. He kicked the wood, cursing. The boots were so thick he didn't feel any pain. Physically, anyway.

So this was it? He was going to be out here until he dug some stupid holes?

"Fine!"

Jason grabbed the post-hole digger. "How hard can it be?" With one big, heaving motion, he plunged it into the earth, barely making a dent. He tried again, this time getting a little further, but was still able to lift only a handful of dirt out of the ground.

"Okay . . ." This was harder than it looked. But he wasn't going to let an old man show him up. It was a hole, for crying out loud. Anybody could dig a hole.

So on he went, even through lunch, which was dropped off by some ranch hands who seemed to enjoy themselves immensely as they drove off waving and hollering.

Much later—he wasn't even sure what time it was—he'd dug eight holes. Lifting the posts, he carried them to the holes and dropped them in. A few leaned a bit sideways, so he moved some dirt around to try to get them to stand as erect as possible. Most of them did.

Standing beside the pile of posts was a reel of wire. Jason looked at the fence posts. Then, grabbing the wire, he tied one end off on the first post and strung the rest around the other poles.

"Yes! Genius! Thank you!" He put his hands on his hips and looked down the upright, albeit slightly crooked, fence line. "There! Take that, Gus! Take that!"

And speaking of Gus, like clockwork, here he came, his truck rumbling down the gravel road. Jason could see his elbow stuck out the window. He slowed down and pulled his truck to the side. Framed by the window, he chewed on a toothpick. Could this guy get any more cliché?

Jason smiled broadly and gestured toward his piece of art, even though he could barely lift his arms. "Eh? Not bad for a city boy." And, just for effect, Jason wiped the sweat off his brow.

He watched Gus back up and turn the truck around. The Texan hopped out. His eyes carefully examined the fence.

"Hey," Jason said. "What do you think?"

Gus didn't look like he was thinking about anything. He ignored Jason as he went to his truck and retrieved some rope.

"What's the rope for?" Jason was feeling generous. "Let me help you."

Gus finally looked at him. "You know how to lasso?"

"Um . . . only with my charm." Jason laughed, hoping to lighten the curmudgeon up a little. But, hey, at least he'd put up a fence.

Gus swung the rope over his head and lassoed the first fence post. Jason folded his arms. "Wow. Maybe if you keep practicing, you can lasso something that moves."

Gus grinned. "Oh, this is going to move all right."

Without another word, he hog-tied the other end of the rope

to his trailer hitch, climbed back into his truck, started the engine, and put it in forward.

Jason stared in disbelief as he watched one fence post after another pop out of the ground and trail behind the pickup truck as it drove away.

"No! Hey! Aw . . . come on, man!"

But everything was quiet again.

Jason stood there. When he was in high school, he'd made boys cry, so he wasn't about to shed a tear. But it took every ounce of willpower to keep his despair in check.

"What do you want from me!" he screamed, but his voice only disappeared into the vast plains around him.

He looked up, pointing his finger straight over his head. "What do you want from me?"

When there was no response, he kicked his boot into the gravel. Then kicked again. And again. Over and over, ten, twelve, fourteen times, until a dust cloud formed around him and he was lost to a paroxysm of coughing.

That was it. He wasn't digging another hole. No gift was worth this.

○ ○ ○

"So . . . I'm dying to know. What did you get?"

Caitlin's voice was patchy at best, but if he stood with one foot on top of the cab of the tractor he was standing on and dipped his right shoulder a little, he could hear her. Glancing up, he noticed

Gus studying him from a second-story window. "Uh, it's complicated, but it involves land, building materials, and slave labor."

"They're giving you a shopping mall?"

Jason dipped his shoulder a little more. "Not exactly."

"So it must be the land, right? They're giving that to you?"

"Uh, land's got a lot to do with it. Yeah."

"You don't sound too sure."

"Well, whatever it is, I gotta survive this geriatric cowboy until he gives it to me. Or when I get back. Or . . ." Jason sighed. "Or when I'm finished . . ."

Wait. That was it? . . . That *was* it! Jason laughed.

"Finish what?"

"You know what? Let me get back to you, okay?"

Jason climbed down from the tractor. Looking through the windows, he could see Gus fiddling with the antennas on his television set. "So that's it." Jason slapped his hands together. Then winced. He was going to have to get an ice pack.

High up on a distant hill, Gus leaned against the door of his truck. The kid had been at it for six hours, working straight through lunch. Gus watched him measure, check, recheck, dig deeper holes, even start over a couple of times. He'd put up fifty-seven fence posts, ten of them today. It was back-breaking work.

And miracle of miracles, he'd actually been showing up to breakfast. *Early*, even.

Gus spit his wad of tobacco out and looked up to the sky. "You know how to pick 'em. I gotta tell ya, I didn't think he had it in him." Chuckling, Gus climbed into his truck and poked a toothpick between his teeth. Driving down the hill, he turned onto the long gravel road that led to the other side of this acreage. One of his crews was busy working on another part of the fence, but Gus waved the three men into his truck. They hopped in and Gus headed toward Mr. Fence.

Jason was busy packing the circumference of a post and didn't notice the truck until he stood up. Gus slowed down and the crew hopped out. Jason watched as one of them picked up a post.

"Let's go," Gus said to Jason.

"I'm not done," the kid said, out of breath.

Gus smiled. "Work's never done on a ranch."

He watched Jason turn toward the fence line, a satisfactory smile emerging on his lips as he took in the view of all he'd accomplished.

"All right. Whatever." He dropped the shovel and climbed into the truck.

Gus turned on Patsy Cline. He was sort of glad this kid wasn't a big talker. There was nothing worse than hearing somebody yak everyone to death.

◇ ◇ ◇

Jason napped on and off until they arrived at the airport.

Gus pulled up to the curb. "You know," he said, turning to look at Jason, "you do any work like you did here, you can do anything."

Jumping out of the truck, Jason grabbed his bag from the back and stood on the sidewalk, staring at Gus. "Now aren't you forgetting something?"

"I don't think so. Shoot."

"The *gift.* I came here to pick up a gift, remember?"

Gus howled. This kid was something else. Likable enough, but a little slow.

Gus gave him a short wave and pulled into the airport traffic. He hated traffic.

chapter 5

*t*hat was the gift?" Jason could hardly contain himself, and it didn't help that Hamilton and Miss Hastings looked completely amused as they sat across from him in the conference room. "I do manual labor for a month, and you're trying to tell me it was a favor? To me?"

"The gift of work," Hamilton said with a glance toward Miss Hastings, as if she might be able to explain it better.

"Wow." Jason looked back and forth between the two of them.

"Congratulations," Hamilton added.

"Look, Hamilton, just tell me what my total inheritance is. I'm over this." He gestured at the room like it was responsible. If he thought it would help, he'd drive his fist through the wall, but then he'd probably have to fix it himself.

But to Jason's surprise, Hamilton stood up to leave. Jason's heart skipped a beat, and he rushed to the other side of the table. "Where are you going?" He glanced at Miss Hastings. "Where is he going? Can you tell him to come back, please?"

Miss Hastings gave him an apologetic shrug as her eyes followed Hamilton out the door. Jason ran after him. "Mr. Hamilton! Mr. Hamilton . . . Hey!" Jason stepped in front of him in the most polite way one can cut someone off. "Mr. Hamilton, sir, please . . ." Jason took a breath. "I think it's only fair that I know the amount of money that we're dealing with here. Don't you?" His voice rose with every word. Hamilton just looked bored. "I mean, I've been gone for a month. Just tell me what do I have to do? What is it?"

"Red said 'a series of gifts.'"

Jason's nostrils flared. The last thing he wanted to do was restrain himself, but something told him smarting off might be a little costly at this point. He looked at the ground, trying to come up with something to say that wouldn't have gotten him slapped by his mother if she were standing nearby.

"Let me add a personal note," Hamilton said. "I, too, think this is a waste of time, but it will end shortly because you are going to fail. I expect you to fail and to fail miserably." Hamilton stepped around him and headed for his office, then stopped. He turned toward Jason. "Now, if you do want to continue, make an appointment with Miss Hastings."

Jason's mind reeled. He didn't want to give up. He glanced at Miss Hastings, who had followed them and was sitting at her desk with perfect posture, attentive eyes, and an expression that made him want to take on the old man.

Jason cleared his throat. "Okay, look, Mr. Hamilton, I've been acting like a moron about this whole thing, and I'm sorry. And now I see exactly what you and Red have in store for me, and I think it's exceedingly beneficial." He actually had to stop and smile at himself. That was good. He looked Hamilton in the eyes. "So what's the next gift?"

"You'll know."

Jason's Charger R/T roared into the parking garage of his apartment building. It shattered any hope of silence, and it always made heads turn, especially when his tires squealed, like they did as he pulled into his reserved parking space at thirty miles per hour.

That was about all the joy he was getting out of life at the moment, and even that was a stretch. But at least he was home. His arm muscles were burning like someone had lit them on fire, but strangely, he was in a good mood. Whistling, even, as he threw his keys up in the air, caught them, and noticed two tow-truck drivers taking a break near the back of their truck.

"Howdy," one of them said.

If he never heard that word again, it wouldn't be too soon.

As he rode the elevator up to his apartment, he wondered how someone could live like Gus had for so many years. He was all for nature, but for him a houseplant and a good view would do. Still, he couldn't help but wonder what Gus did all day long. Build fences? Herd sheep? Milk the cows?

The thought of that kind of life made Jason want to go hug his big-screen TV. Soak in his Jacuzzi. Lie on his leather couch. Heck, he might even treat himself to a massage.

Heck. That was funny. The ghost of Gus, still haunting him. *Just don't say it out loud.* He had a reputation, after all. In some circles, quite a good one too.

He went through a mental checklist of all the things he needed to do today. He wasn't coming up with much, except returning to Hamilton's office this afternoon. Jason wasn't sure why the urgency, but Miss Hastings had said, "You'll be eager to come. I promise."

Yeah, right. Eager. Hardly. But he'd put on a good show.

The elevator doors opened and Jason pulled out his key. He flung open the door to his apartment.

And then, like a punch to the stomach, he lost his breath.

Scrambling back downstairs, he flung open the parking-garage door just in time to see his car being pulled behind the tow truck. "Wait!" He bolted for the iron gate, which was closing as the tow truck turned onto the street. "Wait! That's an eight-thousand-dollar paint job!"

◇ ◇ ◇

Hamilton watched Jason's fingernails dig into the leather armrests of the boardroom chair in which he sat. The dark room held the sounds of Red's laughter from the video screen. Judging from Jason's reaction, Red was lucky he was dead. At the moment, Jason looked like he could kill someone.

Red wiped tears of laughter from his eyes.

Jason had come home to a completely empty apartment, stripped bare of everything that wasn't nailed down. Hamilton wished he could've been there to see his face. But right now his face was doing plenty of emoting.

Finally Red spoke. "Ah, well, you don't begin to live until you've lost everything. Heck, I've lost everything three or four times. It's the perfect place to start." He smiled at the camera.

"For most of your adult life, you have been the life of the party and an easy touch for a lot of weak hangers-on. Now let's see who your real friends are."

Hamilton froze the picture. Jason just stared forward, hardly blinking, almost like he was in shock. Miss Hastings turned on the lights again.

Finally, Jason spoke. "I was at your funeral, and there wasn't a single person there who wasn't on your payroll or didn't have something to gain from your death."

With that, Jason looked calmly at Hamilton. "What exactly is he asking me to do?"

"He wants you to come back at the end of the month with one *true* friend," Hamilton said.

Jason rose and walked out.

Hamilton looked at Miss Hastings. "Why are we even wasting our time?"

"It's what Red wanted," she replied.

Hamilton stared at the frozen image on the screen in front of him. "I hope you know what you're doing."

◇ ◇ ◇

A low hum of conversation surrounded them inside their favorite restaurant, high class and inaccessible to the general public. Jason watched Caitlin devour the food in front of her—with good manners, of course. Jason's food sat untouched on his plate as Caitlin mindlessly talked about her day. She did like to talk. Jason wondered if she would even notice if he got up and walked away. Sometimes he wanted to. It felt like he could drown in her words.

The waiter appeared, a tight grin on his face as he gently fished for compliments. He glanced at Jason's plate, then looked at Caitlin. "And how were the lobster tails?"

"Fine. Thanks."

He tipped the wine bottle over his forearm and poured more wine for Caitlin. But his attention was on Jason. "The lady was enjoying a Montrachet. And, sir, the Margaux. I hope it met your expectations."

"It was terrific. Thank you." Jason sighed. *Go away.*

"We don't get too many requests for the '78. It's a bit too pricey for some of our patrons."

Jason looked up, not bothering to smile.

"I'll just leave this with you now," the waiter said, placing the bill on the table.

"Caitlin, where do you see our relationship?" He dropped his credit card on the tab and the waiter snatched it and left.

Caitlin's eyes, twinkling in the candlelight, widened in expectation. "What are you asking me, Jason Stevens?"

"Just thinking. How long have we been going out?"

"An appropriate amount of time." She brushed several stray wisps of hair off her forehead. "Long enough."

"See? My thoughts exactly. I was thinking that maybe we should begin to take us—" She leaned forward, hanging on his every word.

"—more seriously."

"Yes?"

"But there's something I want to ask you first."

"Jason, if you're talking about a prenup, isn't that sort of passé?"

"Well, see, I was thinking—"

Suddenly the waiter stood above them again. Jason sighed loudly as he looked up.

"Excuse me, sir. The charge card company has declined the charge."

"That's impossible," Jason said. "I don't have a credit limit. Just run it through again."

"It's always our practice to 'run it through again,' but they declined." The waiter's polite tone had taken a serious departure.

Jason pulled out his wallet and threw another card down. "Okay," he continued as the waiter left again, "so I was thinking, um, well . . . Maybe it would be a good time for me to move in with you."

44

Caitlin's chin dropped. "You move in with me? Why? Half my wardrobe's at your penthouse."

Jason threw in a shrug. "It's just for a change of scenery. Besides, I'm remodeling my place."

Caitlin leaned forward. "A remodel? But who's your designer? I know everyone in town."

"I should've said I'm *beginning* to remodel. I've only really started with the demolition—"

There was the waiter again. And this time he was accompanied by the manager. "I'm sorry, sir," the manager said, her voice overly loud, "your bank is on the line. They'd really like to speak with you. I must insist."

"Look, guys," Jason said, lightening his tone and giving the manager a smile, "I'm having a little bit of a setback. It's nothing that can't be fixed, all right?"

He glanced back at Caitlin. She looked mortified. "Sweetie, I'm switching accounts right now, and I'm . . . temporarily out of money. Is there a way you could pay for this?"

Caitlin's expression fell. Like she'd jumped off a cliff. "Jason?" Her tone rose in disbelief. "You're, um . . . you're . . . asking me to pay the bill?"

Jason nodded. Did she have something in her eye or were those actual tears?

Like she'd just heard news of a family member's death, she shoved her chair back, stood, threw her napkin onto the table, slung her purse over her shoulder, and rushed from the room.

Something was definitely dead—including, apparently, his

45

credit line. Luckily, thanks to a lot of charm and namedropping—
including, of all people, Red—the manager agreed to let him go.

As soon as he hit daylight, he flipped open his phone and hit
speed dial.

"Jeff? It's Jason. Listen, I need a favor."

"You need a favor? Ha!" his friend snorted.

"What's so surprising about that?"

"Nothing, man," Jeff said, chuckling. "What do you want?"

"I need to borrow some money."

"You've been drinking!" Jeff laughed outright this time. "I can
tell."

"Jeff, I'm serious. I need to borrow some money."

At this, Jeff was silent.

"You owe me. Dude, I'm rolling over—"

"I can't."

"What do you mean you can't? I've been there for you count-
less times. You owe me! That's it. Bottom line."

"Jason . . . Look, man, I would love to, but I'm not really in a
position to—"

"Who was the one who loaned you ten grand last year?"

"Yeah . . . Like I said, that was for my mom, who was sick in the
hospital . . ."

"You know, I could've come up with a better excuse when I was
twelve years old!" Jason sighed at the silence on the other end.
"All I need is a place to sleep." More silence. "I don't get what the
problem is, dude. You can let me spend the night, *one night*." He
waited but heard nothing. "Hello?"

Another male voice replied. "We're sorry. Your cell phone service has been discontinued. If you think this is an error, please—"

Jason snapped the phone shut and squeezed it tightly in his hand, then slammed it against the concrete. Pieces flew everywhere, and a nearby man scuttled aside with a nasty look.

"Can I help you?" Jason growled. The man hurried his pace. "Yeah. Shut up."

Jason took a deep breath, trying to calm himself down. *Think. Think!* With a longsuffering gaze to the west, he began to walk against busy traffic on the street.

○ ○ ○

On grass nice enough to be carpet, Jason caught his breath. He didn't think of himself as out of shape, especially after his time in Texas, but he felt every inch of his billion-mile walk to his mother's house. At this point he'd even be willing to drive a minivan. Anything to keep from having to walk, like someone from the first century.

The enormous mansion, glowing from the light within, elegant to the point of senselessness, glared down at him. All this for one woman. What did she do with all those rooms?

Lucky for him, she had all those rooms. All he wanted to do was lie down and sleep. He trudged up a driveway so long it deserved to be named a street till he finally reached the front door. Ringing the bell, he could hear the chimes announcing him. He would've just walked in, but he'd made that mistake before. His mother . . . well, she liked men. A lot. And seeing her making out with one on the sofa had been enough to last ten lifetimes. He was definitely permanently scarred, and if he ever had to sue her, he'd bring it up in court and ask for pain-and-suffering money.

The door swung open, and his mother's anticipating eyes suddenly grew round with shock. She slid a hand in front of herself as she secured her silk robe closed. Jason looked away with an eye roll and waited.

"Jason!" she gasped, like he'd been missing for years. "Um . . . what a surprise!" She smiled. Sort of.

Jason started to step around her and into the house. "Mom, you're never going to believe this."

Her hands hit his chest, pushing him back out the door. "I'm afraid I can't let you in," she said.

Standing back out on the porch, Jason stared at her. "I'm having a bit of a situation," he said curtly. "I need some help. I need to borrow some money."

She patted his cheek. "Of course you do. Everyone needs money." She cleared her throat and fixed an awkward gaze on him. "Um, didn't your grandfather leave you anything?"

"What are you talking about? He hated me."

"Jason," she said, putting on her motherly voice, "he did not. He didn't come around much, but I always thought it was because of me." She tightened her robe a little more.

"It doesn't matter. Do you have any extra spending cash?"

"I would love to help you, but I can't."

"You can't?"

"They told me specifically that you would be coming around for money and that I was not to give you anything."

"But I'm your son, Mom. That's what you're supposed to do."

She looked up with pleading eyes. "If I violate their instructions, I am out everything. Everything!"

What was this, the mob?

"So for the sake of the greater good, I must insist that you leave." She jutted her chin up a little. "I'm not gonna upset the whole apple cart just because you're facin' a few challenges. I'm sorry. I just cannot help you."

"Thanks," Jason said as she closed the door in his face.

chapter 6

Jason couldn't believe it, but he'd witnessed yet another sunrise. Well, almost. The maid had found him asleep on one of the poolside chairs and beaten him away with a feather duster. Anyway, the sun at this time of day was spectacularly over rated, if you asked him. But then again, he was in a bad mood. A really bad mood.

With his legs crossed at the ankles and his arms crossed at his chest, he stared at nature. Birds pooping all over the place. Dogs sniffing each other's backsides. Women jogging who looked like they'd rather be dead.

And then there was him. Not that anybody had noticed or cared, but he was, apparently, homeless. No, that was too harsh of a word. Well, maybe not. He'd actually spent the night outside, and it wasn't because he was camping.

Think. There had to be a solution. A way out of this. Some way he could outsmart Hamilton.

His stomach grumbled loudly enough that he glanced around. He was alone, to his disappointment. Maybe it was him, but it seemed like people were avoiding eye contact with him. Not that he cared, but it seemed weird. Or maybe he was just being paranoid.

And he was cold. Who knew mornings could be so cold? There was dew on the grass, but the air smelled kind of clean. Crisp. Whoopee.

"Hey, man. You're . . . you're on my bench. On my bench."

The man standing over him looked like Jason felt. And smelled like Jason looked, after a weekend of partying. He looked like a chimney sweeper.

"Beat it," Jason told him.

"A simple no would have sufficed."

Sufficed? Where'd this guy come from? Maybe he was one of those investors his uncles talked about who went berserk when the stock market plunged.

"Fine. *No.*"

"No, what?"

"No, you cannot sit on this bench. This is not your bench. This is a city bench," Jason said, gesturing toward the park to help the guy get a clue. "Go sit on another bench." He pitched a thumb sideways to the two additional benches that sat less than five feet away.

"But it's my bench, you know?" The guy was kind of whiny.

"I've got just as much right to it as anybody. It's a free country, you know."

"See," Jason said, anger bubbling, "that's where you're wrong. Name one thing in this country that's for free. You need money for everything. Without money, you're nothing. Look at you. No money. No food. No family. No friends. Nothing. Besides, I'm sitting on this bench now. This is my bench. Okay?"

The man didn't look the slightest bit deterred. "I'll flip you for it."

Jason rolled his eyes. "Fine," he said. Standing, he drove his hands into his pockets, searching for a coin. So did the bum. At the same moment, they realized neither one of them had a coin.

"I have a quarter."

Jason whipped around to find a child standing there holding an umbrella. Why was she holding an umbrella? It was bright and sunny. And why was she offering money to two grown men she didn't know? She stuck out her hand and offered Jason the quarter.

"Uh . . . thanks."

Jason turned to the bum and smirked. The bum smirked back. Jason flipped the coin high in the air. But as he waited for it to fall again, the bum suddenly snatched it midair and took off running.

Whatever. Jason flopped down on *his* bench.

"Well, aren't you going to chase him for it?"

"Beat it, kid."

"I've been watching you," the girl continued. She had an irritatingly mature way about her. Sort of like a miniature mother. Her disapproving eyes studied him. "You're not a real bum. I saw you at a funeral."

His eyes blinked open. "What were you doing at the—"

"My mother and I come here for lunch every day. Except right now, she doesn't know where I am."

Her self-satisfied smile was broken by yelling, which made Jason jump and the little girl roll her eyes like a teenager.

"Emily! Emily!" A woman came tearing across the grass toward them, her eyes frantically glued to Jason.

"Whatever," the girl sighed. She looked at Jason as though nobody was calling her name. "You must really be having a bad life."

The woman, apparently the girl's mother, charged toward her, now in a full-fledged stomp, relief replacing fear. "Come on. Right now." She glanced at Jason, somewhat apologetically, and took her daughter by the shoulders, trying to move her in the opposite direction.

But Emily didn't budge. She looked at her mother with one hand on her hip. "I was just having a pleasant conversation with this gentleman. Leave us alone, please."

"Dear, don't be ridiculous," the mother said, embarrassment washing over her face as she looked at Jason. "Sorry to disturb you."

"That's okay. I'm not the one who's disturbed."

Emily looked indignant. "Some friend you are. Thanks a lot, poser."

Finally, the mother guided her away, lecturing in her ear about stranger danger. But Jason couldn't help himself. Like someone else at the controls, he followed them. How creepy could he get? Maybe not as creepy if he tried to smile and look normal. Didn't he look normal? Surely.

"Hey," Jason said, calling after them.

The mother quickly turned, pulling her daughter toward her.

Jason held up his hands and tried a kind voice. "Wait . . . wait, wait." He took a few steps closer. The mother's eyes widened. "Okay, this is going to sound really, really strange, but I'm just going to come out and say it. I'll make a deal with you. I need a friend, but only for a little while, and, uh, in return, I don't know . . ." Jason looked up, searching for something he could give away. "I'll take you both to Disney World!" Yeah. That was good. Of course, he couldn't do that now, but later, when he got this mess sorted out.

The mother leaned forward and narrowed her eyes. "Excuse me?"

"I need a friend," Jason said again. Maybe he needed to look more desperate. That probably didn't need to be feigned.

The mother began glancing around nervously, obviously hoping to catch the attention of a jogger or maybe even a bum. Anybody but him. Emily, however, looked intrigued. She slipped out of her mother's grasp and put her hand back on her hip. "Explain yourself," she said.

Jason paused. How could he explain this? "It's complicated." The mother gave him an *I'll bet* look that could've melted iron.

·"No. It's not. It's pathetic," Emily said. She stared him down, just like her mother, and then they both turned back and began walking toward the hospital.

"Okay . . ." Jason sighed for what must've been the eightieth time in an hour. Throwing up his arms, he turned to go sit on his bench. "Oh, dude. Come on."

The bum sat smiling on the bench, flipping his quarter through his fingers.

◇ ◇ ◇

He'd been chased by a dog from Caitlin's backyard, scaling the iron gate to avoid the fierce, snapping jaws of the Rottweiler. But a bite out of his flesh might've felt better than watching the scene now before him. He'd located Caitlin having the time of her life. Through the security fence of the Gaylord home, Jason watched Caitlin enjoying herself over a glass of wine and a plate full of flirt. She kissed Daniel and giggled. *Daniel,* of all people. The guy snorted every time he laughed and didn't even know how to drive a stick shift.

Jason didn't have to turn around to know that the neighborhood security guard was about to involve himself. Clinging to the wrought iron fence, Jason watched Caitlin lose herself in the moment.

The security guard came up beside him and, with Jason, observed the two through the window. He seemed to sense Jason's pain. Temporarily. Then he grabbed Jason by the shirt and led him toward a patrol car. Jason gestured toward them and their oblivion.

"You know, she doesn't even *like* Chateau Montrachet?

o o o

"Miss Hastings," Hamilton said, "bring me the Stevens file. Looks like our boy's not even going to make it through round two."

She stepped toward his desk, clasping her hands together. "But, sir. Doesn't he have until the *end* of today?"

Hamilton looked up, raising an eyebrow. "Well, from what I hear, he could have another month and still get the same result."

Miss Hastings looked down. She knew Hamilton was a skeptic; that was practically part of his title. But something told her Jason just needed a little more time. Maybe she could talk to Hamilton, convince him to give the boy at least another day or two. Jason wasn't brimming with maturity, but she was starting to think he might be catching on to the idea.

"The Stevens file?"

"Yes, sir."

chapter 7

Jason awoke. The first thing he saw was a bright blue sky. *Finally.* He'd missed the sunrise. Things might be on their way to normal again.

With his hands tucked under his armpits, he tried not to shiver. But his chattering teeth were doing a good job of reminding him that sleeping on a bench outside in the middle of a park was far from normal.

He tried to doze back to sleep but then heard a commotion. A woman yelling. Sitting up, he turned around to find the little girl he'd met yesterday with her umbrella. Except she wasn't holding it over her head—she was jabbing it toward that stupid bum, who had tried to steal his bench *once again* last night when nature came calling. The mother was yelling something about 911 and holding her phone up in the air as if it might detonate a bomb. Apparently they were defending Fort Picnic.

To Jason's surprise, they seemed to be holding their own. Emily didn't look frightened, but rather annoyed. Her mother kept threatening to use the cell phone to make a call, but Jason thought she might actually throw it at the guy. All this while dodging the bum's attempts to snatch lunch.

The bum managed to grab a bag of chips, except he didn't look like he wanted the chips. Maybe he wanted the PB&J.

"Hey . . . hey . . ." the mother said, stretching her arm out to hold him off. "Give that—sir, you need to step back." The bum grabbed for the entire lunch basket but missed. "Hey! I've got 911 all dialed in!" she shouted. "All I have to do is press *Send*. See? See?" She quickly moved Emily behind her. "Sweetheart, get back."

"Hey! Hey!" Jason ran toward them. "Leave 'em alone!"

The bum turned, and to Jason's surprise, started running . . . toward Jason. Which caused Jason to come to a screeching halt and wonder if he was going to have to dial back his memory to fifth grade when he'd taken karate.

Even with the little limp he had, the bum clipped along toward Jason at a good pace.

"Oh . . . no you don't!" Jason quickly turned, rushing back to his bench and planting his rear on the wood. The bum stopped and sighed. Jason reclined and smirked. "My bench."

Grumbling, the bum skulked away. Jason looked at the

mother, who was kissing Emily and, to Jason's delight, looking pretty grateful.

"Thanks," she said.

"You're welcome."

She stuck out her hand. "I'm Alexia. This is Emily."

"We've met," Emily said, putting the umbrella back over her head.

Alexia smoothed her hair and tucked her cell phone away. "Well . . . um . . ." She glanced down at the picnic basket. "Maybe, uh . . ."

"I would love to."

○ ○ ○

Jason had been forced to attend etiquette school when he was in third grade. His mother had been big on it. Something about how all his other cousins ate like pigs, burped at the table, and acted, in general, like heathens and idiots. So he learned to chew with his mouth closed, use the correct utensil, and fold his napkin in his lap.

Except now he was stuffing an entire peanut butter and jelly sandwich into his mouth. His cheeks bulged on each side, and he barely had enough room to chew. Gulping it down as fast as he could without choking, he felt only slight embarrassment as Alexia and Emily watched him like he was a monkey at the zoo. Between chews, he was attempting an explanation for how he'd gotten himself into this mess.

"So," Emily said, those scrutinizing, mother-like eyes watching him at every moment. "You have a bet with a dead guy?"

Jason nodded, glancing at Alexia.

"Cool." Emily smiled.

Yeah, not so cool, but that was another story.

Alexia patted Emily on the shoulder. "Emily, be polite." But she looked equally as curious. "Wait, how can you have a bet with a deceased person?"

"See, that's the part that's complicated," Jason said, sitting back and letting the food rest in his stomach.

"So you come up with a friend. What do you get if we go along with this?"

"Emily!" Alexia said, embarrassment trickling into her tone.

"No, it's okay," he said. He'd be curious too. In fact, this whole thing would be rather amusing if it weren't happening to him. "I don't know. Something about an ultimate gift. Or something."

"But you're not sure what that is?" Emily was asking all the adult questions. Alexia looked like she was restraining herself to not look eagerly interested.

"Yeah. That about sums it up."

"So what do we get if we agree to do this? We need money. How much are you willing to pay?"

"Emily!" Alexia shook her head and glanced apologetically at Jason. "I'm sorry. You're going to have to excuse my daughter. Sometimes she tends to be a little outspoken."

Jason gazed at Emily. He was beaten. She was smart, savvy, and had his number. "I can't promise you anything," he said to Emily.

"Now that's better." She smiled as if she'd just conquered him, then she placed a can of soda in front of him. "But what if we really *did* become friends?"

◇ ◇ ◇

Hamilton sat comfortably in one of twelve leather conference room chairs that encircled a table. Jason slouched with his knee against it. And this little girl, though cute enough, was sucking the life out of a soda can and wasn't about to begin anything until she finished. He glanced back at Miss Hastings, who looked hopeful.

He was skeptical. The mother of the young girl didn't know whether to sit back and let it all unfold or sit forward and help both Jason and this girl with their manners.

The little girl, who had introduced herself as Emily, looked a little familiar. Hamilton couldn't place her, though. And that wasn't his concern now. Emily finished off her soda with the loudest slurping sound he'd ever heard.

The mother couldn't stand it any longer. She leaned forward. "Emily, it's not polite to—"

Hamilton held a hand up. It was time to get down to business. "So you're Jason's friend?"

Emily sat up tall, folded her arms on top of the table, and looked him right in the eye. "Yes, I am."

"True friend?"

"Absolutely. Pinky promise."

Hamilton could hear Miss Hastings snicker behind him. "So how long have you known Mr. Stevens?"

"We go *way* back. We're like this." She held up her hand, twisting her middle finger around her pointer finger. "Now, where do I sign?"

Hamilton leaned forward, engaging the girl with a serious tone and sharp eyes that didn't affect her at all. "And, he hasn't promised you any compensation for this friendship?"

The girl gestured toward Jason, who still hadn't managed to undo the slouch he was so fond of. "Look at him." Everyone did. "Does he look like he has anything to offer?"

Miss Hastings let out a chuckle. Everyone in the room looked as though they agreed. Jason finally sat up a little and ran a hand through hair that looked in bad need of a shower.

"So, do you expect," Hamilton asked, "this friendship to continue?"

"I plan on knowing Jason for the rest of my life." Suddenly the girl stood. "Now, where do I sign?"

Hamilton sighed, pushing the paper forward. They all watched as she carefully wrote her name on the bottom line, complete with a heart over the *i* and a squiggly tail at the end of the *y*. Then she unfurled her umbrella, nearly hitting Hamilton in the face with it. The mother looked ready to die of embarrassment

Jason, on the other hand, looked like he could burst into song and dance.

"Thank you for your time, Miss Emily," Hamilton said, shaking her hand.

She marched out the door, her exasperated mother trailing. Jason followed, but not without a satisfied smirk.

◊ ◊ ◊

Outside the office building, Alexia said good-bye to Jason. "Tomorrow. Lunch at noon. Our usual spot in the park," Emily told him.

"Sure," Jason said, his tone giving away his insincerity.

"Just a minute, pal!" Emily said, her face drawn into a fierce scowl. "You owe me!"

But he was walking away, leaving them both staring after him incredulously. To his retreating back, Emily made a gesture: three fingers up, out, and then an L. "Whatever, loser!"

Alexia watched the guy walk off. Emily stormed the other direction. "Emily, wait . . ." Alexia was sort of inclined to make the gesture herself.

◊ ◊ ◊

Having nothing better to do, Jason headed back to the conference room, but it was empty. The coffeepot wasn't. He poured himself a cup, loaded plenty of sugar into it, and guzzled.

For the first time, across the waiting area, he noticed a photograph. He wandered over to take a look. He wasn't sure he'd ever seen Hamilton smile, but there he was grinning it up with Red.

Behind him, he heard Miss Hastings's heels clicking across the floor. Standing next to him, she observed the photos with him.

"They go back a long way, don't they?"

Miss Hastings, quiet for a moment, nodded slightly. Then in a soft voice she said, "There was a time when Mr. Hamilton was quite ill and needed a kidney transplant. Your grandfather went out of his way to help him find a donor. You could even say, I think, that Mr. Hamilton's alive today because of Red Stevens."

Jason noticed Miss Hastings leaning in toward him. She cleared her throat, and Jason could only hope she wasn't about to spill some family secret or dish out dirt on Red. Well, he supposed he could stand to hear that, but that probably wasn't likely to happen. "In the, um, basement of this building, there is a small apartment for a custodian." She glanced behind her and lowered her voice even more. "It isn't being used right now. Perhaps you'd, um, like to take a look at it?"

chapter 8

hamilton resisted the urge to stare at the kid instead of staring at the video of Red. Somehow he'd managed to get a shower. Yesterday, Miss Hastings had done her best to neutralize the place with air freshener, but even this morning a strange odor still lurked. At the moment it was replaced by some cheap drugstore cologne Jason just might've bathed in, but Hamilton kept his mouth shut.

He wanted Jason concentrating on the video. And he was. He seemed drawn in with every word that Red spoke.

"Jason," Red said, "you have no concept whatsoever of the value of money. Money has always been available to you like the air you breathe. Let's stop and review some highlights of your recent past."

Jason glanced nervously at Hamilton, guilt washing over his face.

"A twenty-five-*thousand*-dollar-per-night suite in Paris with a personal chef, whom you tipped heavily."

Jason shrugged.

"A tour of the Bordeaux region in chauffeured hot-air balloons?" Red looked truly baffled.

Jason smiled at the memory. "That was amazing."

"A week of heli-skiing in San Moritz. A small fleet of exotic cars," Red continued.

A twinge of pain passed across Jason's face as he apparently recalled the repossession.

"The latest in everything. Including women." Red paused with a wry smile. "But the past is the past, and I figure you've probably had a pretty tough month."

Jason's eyes widened at the apparent sympathy Red was showing through the video. Hamilton handed Jason an envelope. His expression brightened immediately.

"Well, it's about time!" He glanced between Hamilton and Miss Hastings as he stood up, waving the envelope in the air with a smile. "Thank you very much. And if I ever see you two again, it will be too soon." With a bounce in his step, he ushered himself out of the room. Hamilton actually thought he could hear him humming.

Miss Hastings looked sympathetic. "I feel sorry for him."

"Please," Hamilton growled. "Don't feel sorry for him. He doesn't deserve that."

"But he's coming along."

"He has a long way to go."

Hamilton got comfortable in his seat. There was no use going back to his office.

And not a minute later, Jason came stomping back into the conference room. The envelope had been torn, along with the optimism he'd carried out of the room. Without a word, he threw the envelope down and plunged himself back into his chair. A heavy silence engulfed the room. Hamilton resumed the video.

"Well, seeing how you've never held one of those before, let me explain what it is. That's a paycheck. For what you earned at Gus's ranch." Rage built in his tone. "'Course, the IRS ravaged it first. I hate those guys. In your pocket every step of the way. You start out in business and then you have to make a payroll, and just when you think you're going to make—"

A voice, somewhere behind the camera, cut Red off. "Mr. Stevens . . . this is the gift of money, please?"

"Yeah, right. Sorry. Look at me," he said with a laugh. "I'm carrying on about death and taxes even after I'm dead! You have to take that money, and as much as you need it yourself, spend it on someone experiencing a real problem."

A sigh like a howling wind came from Jason.

"What can they teach you? Put yourself in their shoes."

Hamilton paused the video and swiveled around to look at Jason, the poster boy for dejection. "Jason, would you like us to cash it for you?"

"Please." Jason slid it across the table, looking unamused.

"I think we know you well enough that we won't need any ID," Hamilton said.

"How will you know how I spent it?" Jason asked.

Hamilton smiled. The kid was a little slow. "We'll know."

◇ ◇ ◇

Jason loathed this place. Truthfully, he'd never liked parks at all. Even as a kid. Of course, every time he'd gone it was with a nanny and a handful of other rich kids' nannies. It was hard making friends when the nanny was always breathing down his neck about what kinds of kids he could talk to. Finally, he'd just given up on the park, mostly because his mother had an entire full-sized playground, along with a sandpit and three swing sets, put in behind the house.

Jason scanned the park. The bench, the one he'd share with the bum, was now filled with a couple who didn't have a clue what happened there at night. They were stroking each other's faces and carrying on like it wasn't public property.

Sighing, Jason looked toward the jogging path. Surely that stupid bum was around here somewhere. He was always around.

He stuffed his hands in his pockets, touching the crisp bills with his fingers. His mother always said she loved the way money smelled, but Jason could only imagine how many other people's sweaty hands had touched it before him, which is why he always used a credit card. Well, one of the reasons.

There! The bum! Over by the fountain. His back was to Jason

and he was hunched over something, looking pretty busy for a homeless person.

Reaching into his pocket, Jason pulled out his wad of cash and plucked a hundred-dollar bill from it. For someone who lived by quarters, this could quite possibly be more than the guy could take. Jason smiled, wondering what the bum would do when he saw it . . . when he saw it being *offered* to him.

Jason strolled toward him, hardly able to hide his grin. Yeah, okay, so this felt good. It would feel better if he had his life back, but he would take what he could get. He stood only a few feet away from the bum now, who didn't seem to notice anybody nearby.

"Hey."

The bum whipped around, his back stiffening and his eyes going wide. Jason was just about to tell him to chill when he noticed what the bum was clutching. A purse.

"Hey!"

"I didn't take anything! Nothing."

Throwing the purse down, he fled the scene. He reached down and gathered up several folded pieces of paper that had slid out. He could tell immediately they were hospital bills, and that several of them were stamped with red ink. Past Due.

There was another piece of paper, a rent-due letter. As gently as possible, as if that mattered, he reached in and pulled out the wallet. The driver's license was stuck into a see-through pocket. Alexia. "Oh, no. Great."

He opened the rent due notice: sixteen hundred dollars.

The check he'd received from Gus's farm was for fifteen hundred.

He turned toward the large medical complex that loomed over the park. He hated parks. But he hated hospitals even more.

◇ ◇ ◇

"THE RED STEVENS WING." Large red letters stared him down from outside the elevator.

"Naturally," Jason said aloud to no one in particular.

He stepped out of the elevator, cupping the purse in his hand, trying to look like he wasn't attached to the thing. He turned the corner, and in front of him stretched a massive hallway filled with doors. Sick people. Sick kids. A young girl wearing an outrageous hat passed him by, smiling. The mother only nodded.

Jason took a deep breath. He wasn't sure he wanted to know why Alexia was here. He walked slowly, looking at each door, wondering how he would find her.

A nurse glanced up from the file she was scanning. "Can I help you?"

"Looking for a young blonde woman and her little girl." Jason held out his hand at about the height Emily would be.

"Two doors down," the nurse said.

Jason could see it from where he stood. Hanging on the door was a cheerfully decorated sign reading "Emily's Room." Beneath it was a skull-and-crossbones emblem, accompanied by the words "Keep Out." There was no doubt who'd put that up.

He peeked around the doorframe. Emily was in bed, her eyes lowered and concentrating on something she was reading. Beside her was a mannequin head . . . and the dark hair resting on top of it. Monitors squawked and beeped like they were talking to each other. *Chemo.*

Emily hadn't looked up, so Jason slowly put the purse on the sink next to the door and slid his arm quietly out of the room. Taking a deep breath, he tried to gain his composure. He walked briskly down the hallway, avoiding eye contact. Not that anyone would necessarily recognize him as Red Stevens's grandson, but he didn't want to take any chance—

"What are you doing here?"

Jason tried not to look shocked or shaken or surprised, but he had a feeling all of it was rolling across his face in waves. And by the look on Alexia's face, she was reading it loud and clear.

"You saw her."

Come clean. "Yeah."

"Did you talk to her?"

A litany of excuses offered a hand, but Jason could tell none of them would fly with this woman. So he shook his head. "So what's wrong with her?"

"It depends."

"On what?"

"On who you really are."

"Maybe I can help you."

Alexia's stare bore into him. Her eyes held unquestionable strength. "Emily has leukemia. We thought she was in remission after a bone-marrow transplant, but a couple of weeks ago her body started to reject the transplant." She said it matter-of-factly, like a doctor would, but her eyes betrayed her.

"I'm sorry," Jason said. He wondered how a woman could look so strong and so vulnerable all at the same time. Part of him wanted to reach out and hug her, but he had a feeling that it wouldn't be received, and he wasn't sure he would be good at it anyway.

Her face filled with disappointment, and she walked swiftly past him and around a corner. Jason squeezed his eyes shut. Nothing was going like it was supposed to, and now he'd managed to upset her. She could see right through him.

"Hey . . ."

Alexia stopped, looked up at the ceiling like she was hoping patience might fall upon her, then turned around to look at him.

"You're going to need money, right?"

"Oh, so that's it." Her hand went to her hip. "You won your bet with your rich grandfather and you're back off the streets. Congratulations. What is it now?"

"I do have to give away some money."

She didn't look impressed. "You're getting less mysterious by the minute. I bet you're going to get to the end of your game, collect your cash, and just ride off into the sunset."

"I don't know. Maybe. But, Alexia, if I can help you, why won't you just let me?"

"Because no rich kid is gonna use me or my daughter to play a game."

He could see the hurt in her eyes, but he turned and walked away, heading for the elevator, this time with his back to Red's name. Inside his pocket, he felt for the cash. The elevator doors opened and down he went.

In the lobby, though, he couldn't get himself to leave. Alexia was at the very least suspicious of his motives, so how was he supposed to get her to take this money? He knew it would help her, but she didn't want his help.

Nearby, Jason noticed a man looking at him. And now he'd slid a newspaper in front of his face. Jason sighed. This guy was a terrible spy, but maybe he could serve a purpose. Walking over to him, he snatched the paper out of his hands. The man's eyes went wide with surprise, especially when Jason slapped all the money into his hand.

"She owes sixteen hundred dollars in back rent," Jason said. "Pay it."

"You're a hundred dollars short. Your check was for fifteen hundred."

"Tell Hamilton I'm good for it. Just pay that bill."

◇ ◇ ◇

Hamilton rocked back and forth in his office chair. After all these years it still had that squeak. His thumbs traced the leather armrests. He remembered the day he had bought this chair. It was Christmastime.

"Go out and get yourself a chair, Theophilus!" Red had said at their annual Christmas party. Red usually called him Hamilton. But every once in a while, when he was in a good mood and had some wine down him, he'd call him Theophilus.

"A chair, sir?"

"For your desk."

"I already have a chair."

Red had chuckled. "You have an old wooden chair that looks like it could fall apart at any second."

"It's holding together well enough."

"It squeaks when you move a muscle."

Hamilton had gotten a good laugh out of that. Indeed, it did squeak. When he was taking a phone call he often had to stand up just so the thing wouldn't interrupt.

"Go out and get yourself a nice chair. Leather. Genuine leather, Theophilus. That's the only kind to get. Make it a nice one."

So he did. He'd found the nicest chair he could and had it shipped to the office. They wheeled it in like it was royalty. Miss Hastings had left him to try it out on his own, and he'd backed into it with care. Red was right. It was divine, and maybe it would help his back too.

But as soon as he swiveled, it squeaked. They tried everything to get that chair to stop squeaking, but they never could, and Red had laughed so hard about it, it became an ongoing joke.

The chair was going on fifteen years now.

"Sir," Miss Hastings said over the intercom. "He's coming up."

Hamilton clutched both armrests and pushed himself into a standing position. Shuffling across the floor with his cane, he wondered why Jason had insisted on seeing him this morning. It was early, for one thing, and from what he'd observed so far, the kid didn't rise before lunch. Maybe he was coming to give up. That would sure be a load off his back. Hamilton could get on with business, and he had a lot of it with Red's passing.

Hamilton joined Miss Hastings in the conference room when Jason came strolling through the doors holding a paper sack. Before anyone could say anything, he was dumping the contents onto the middle of the conference room table. Dollar bills and every kind of coin spilled out with a clatter.

"Your other hundred," Jason said. His eyes were intense, his smile satisfied.

Hamilton had to admit, he was impressed. He hadn't thought the kid was that resourceful.

Jason gestured toward the television. "Push *Play*."

Red popped onto the screen and Jason took a seat, leaning forward with an eagerness that Hamilton hadn't witnessed until now.

"Our lives should be lived not avoiding problems, but welcoming them as challenges that will strengthen us so that we can be victorious in the future. So now that I've given you the gift of work, friends, and the value of money, let's discover the gift of family."

Jason's mouth dropped open. Hamilton couldn't blame him. To say his family was problematic was an understatement.

"Now, this is a tough one, but see if it's even remotely possible to get something positive out of our family. See if they truly know how to count their blessings." Red smiled. "If my doctors

75

are remotely accurate, this assignment might even fall on Thanksgiving. How appropriate."

Hamilton paused the video. It was Thanksgiving week. The room was quiet for a moment until Jason looked up at him, desperation in his eyes.

"He's joking, right?"

Hamilton gently shook his head. This was just plain cruel. Going over to the family house, which Hamilton had made the mistake of doing more than once, was like walking into a viper's nest. Red had once invited him for Thanksgiving, insisted that he come, saying it would be a good time. When Hamilton had walked through the ten-foot-high front door, Red was there to greet him. Shaking his hand heartily, Red chuckled. "I lied right through my teeth. This is going to be the worst experience of your life, but I had to get you here to save my sanity. And the turkey is going to be delicious."

It was all true. The meal was extravagant and the best he'd ever had, but the company left a lot to be desired. It all started with who should say the prayer and ended with four people stomping off and a distant aunt pouring gravy into Jack's lap.

Afterward, Red walked Hamilton to his car. "Well, sir, thank you for dinner," Hamilton said.

"Stop it. It was a terrible time." He gazed toward the mansion. Warm light glowed through every one of its windows, but it felt like the coldest place on earth. "Something went wrong. Somewhere I went wrong. How did they all turn out hating each other so much? They have everything they need. Everything."

Red patted Hamilton on the arm but didn't look him in the eye. "Well, good night."

Red stuffed his hands in his pockets and slowly walked back toward the house, like every step killed a little bit more time away from what was inside. It was one of the saddest things he'd ever seen.

"I've got to go," Jason said suddenly and stood up. Without another word he left the room, and Hamilton went back to his squeaky chair.

chapter 9

Part of him wanted to snatch a letter or two off the wall. "ED TEVENS." Yeah. That would be funny.

He sighed. Not even a little bit of mischief would make things better. Which was saying a lot, since it usually provided for some light entertainment when things got dull.

He didn't really know what he was doing back in the Red Stevens wing of the hospital. But here he was.

And he didn't know what he was going to say once he saw her. His heart raced as he followed the same path to Emily's room. He was prepared for a fight. Alexia wasn't going to be happy when she saw him. But he would stand his ground.

What was his ground, anyway?

Ignoring the "Keep Out" sign, he entered her room, only to find a dark-skinned, ample-figured nurse smoothing the bed covers.

"Hey, where's the girl?"

The nurse looked annoyed that she was going to have to stand upright and address him. "Who, Emily? She's with God."

Jason swallowed, scraping his fingers over his scalp. Why had he been such a fool? Why hadn't he come back yesterday? Made things right then? Why hadn't he gone into her room? Said hello to her? He pressed his fingers to his temple, trying to squeeze out all the regrets.

"Don't go all weepy on me. I meant the chapel. Down the hall on your right."

All his emotions came to a screeching halt. "You're kidding me."

"No, but what I wouldn't have given to see you boo-hooing all over the place."

"She told you about me."

The nurse smiled slightly. "Only the part about you being a moron."

Jason went back to the hallway, briskly walking toward the chapel. He found it at the end. It was small, dark, lit only with candles. A miniature version of a life-size chapel.

There was no doubt Red had had his hand in this. He always liked church, kept insisting everybody else should too. "If you don't like the sermon," he would say, "then stare at the stained glass. Sometimes that can say more than words."

The stained glass here seemed to hover over Emily, tiny against the large statue of Jesus that overpowered the room. His arms were outstretched, but he didn't comfort Jason. He looked cold and impersonal. Jason drew his eyes away from the statue and concentrated on Emily.

She sat very still, staring at something in front of her, maybe the statue, maybe the candlelight. Jason stepped farther into the room. She glanced back, then quickly looked away.

"Oh. There's my best friend." That was a lot of sarcasm coming out of such a small body.

Jason walked softly and slid into the pew behind her. Biting his lip, he tried to find the right words. "Listen, about the other day . . ."

"So now you know all about me. No more mysteries."

"Look, I'm really sorry—"

"Shut up. Don't be pathetic."

Jason sat back, holding in whatever his brain thought should come out of his mouth next.

Emily broke the silence. "I wonder if he takes advance orders."

Jason glanced up at the statue. "For what?"

"For my place. You know, up there." She looked up at the ceiling.

Jason exhaled, trying not to look uncomfortable. "What do you think it's going to be like?"

She glanced at him, and for once, Jason let his guard down. There was no use having it up. She saw right through him anyway. "Butterflies," she said. "Lots of butterflies. Did you know God paints every color on a butterfly with his fingers?"

"I didn't know you thought about stuff like that."

"I think about dying." She looked up into the face of the statue. "There's something basically unfair about a person dying. I even hate the idea."

Jason heard the sob that caught in Emily's throat and let his gaze fall to his lap. He couldn't imagine what she was going through. And it broke his heart to know she feared it. He supposed he thought little kids who were going to die had some sort of magic peace about it. But to fear it. To hate it. Just like he did . . . Except she was living it. He only imagined it.

The statue, looming over them both, didn't look cold anymore, but instead, illuminated by candlelight and Emily's sense that it was more than stone, seemed warm with life.

"You know, I don't know much about God," Jason said, staring into the eyes of the statue. "Or Jesus. But I can promise you that those arms are meant for you."

"What's going to happen to my mom? I really don't hate her, you know."

Tears dripped down Emily's face. Her sobs seemed to be the only childlike thing about her, for in her eyes there was a wisdom that stretched far beyond her years.

He rose and went to sit on the pew next to her. He'd never held a child before. Had rarely touched one. But looking into the eyes of Jesus and at the wide-open arms that beckoned all who stood beneath, Jason knew that he was supposed to close the gap by wrapping his own arms around her.

And he did.

It was awkward at first. Her body was stiff with grief, and Jason didn't know whether to hold her tighter or let her go. But then, inch by inch, she relaxed, letting her head lay against his chest. Her small hands clutched his arms.

Jason touched her cheek and held her close. Wasn't he supposed to be the strong one? Yet even as he held her, something told him she was stronger.

After a while she pulled away and looked at him, brushing the tears off her cheek. "Did I mention I wouldn't be upset if you kissed her?"

A surprised laugh erupted from Jason. "Do you think . . . your mom and I . . . ?"

"Okay, it's official," she said, shaking her head like he was a nuisance. "You are the slowest person I have ever met. You two were made for each other. I knew that back in the park."

"In the park I looked like a bum."

"Let's not be delusional. You were a bum."

Jason glanced up at the statue. *I could use some help right now.*

"So," Emily said, turning to him, "what are you doing for Thanksgiving?"

◊ ◊ ◊

"Mrs. Drummond?"

Alexia turned from the counter at the nurses' station.

"I want to send Emily's charts and blood work off to a specialist," Dr. Allen said. "See whether or not she's a candidate for another transplant." His words were sterile, like usual, but this time his eyes showed a deep sadness, and that scared Alexia.

Alexia's mind raced, trying to remember everything every doctor had told her, trying to remember the statistics, the side effects, the other options, but it all seemed a blurred mess inside her head. All she could see was her baby girl, wrapped in a pink blanket, rocked in the warmth and comfort and safety of her mother's arms.

"I'll always protect you," Alexia had said in that early morning when Emily had entered her life. "I will never let anything hurt you."

Dr. Allen cleared his throat, and Alexia tried to take in a deep breath. "Oh. Will that give her a better chance than chemo?"

"Unfortunately, chemotherapy isn't going to be enough. I'm sorry." Dr. Allen squeezed her elbow but couldn't look her in the eye. He grabbed the chart off the counter and disappeared down the corridor.

Alexia wanted to collapse onto her knees, scream at the top of her lungs, hit him. But there she stood, composed, nodding, swallowing back every vicious word that wanted to escape out of her mouth.

Over the many months she'd spent here, she'd watched this scene play out many times. She and Emily would be returning from lunch or a walk or a short trip to the mall, and she would see the doctor, the mom and dad, standing nearby, and by the looks on their faces, she knew it wasn't good news. Averting her eyes, and Emily's attention, she would walk past them, telling herself that it wouldn't be them.

But now it was them.

"No . . ." Alexia covered her mouth, trying to hold it all in, trying to go back to the time when they were safe, together, just the two of them. A horrible pain radiated through her stomach. She clutched it, bent forward, and could hold it in no longer. Every moment they had ever shared together swept through her mind like a wind gust, gone in an instant, replaced by a flood of regret that she hadn't taken the most out of every moment. Why hadn't she rocked her longer? Held her more? Why had laundry been so important on those days when Emily had begged her to go to Chuck E. Cheese? Why had socks on the floor and water out of the bathtub made her lose her temper? Made her yell? So much time wasted. So many minutes thrown out, and now she couldn't get them back. She couldn't get any of it back . . .

"No!" she sobbed. "No . . ."

She barely noticed as Jason rounded the corner of the nurses' station and reached out to support her. Emotions rolled through her like the fierce wave of an angry ocean. She clutched him, bore her fingers into his skin, hated him with everything in her, but she couldn't stand on her own, and the only person holding her up was the most pathetic man she had ever met.

She buried her face into his chest. What she would give if money could take this all away. Her own life. Anything.

But no amount of money could buy Emily a miracle.

◇ ◇ ◇

The diner had become a familiar place. They sat across from one another, and there was a strange comfort in being there with another person. Even if it was Jason. He seemed a little different from before. Maybe it was just the fact that he wasn't talking much, which was a good thing.

Alexia stirred her coffee, watching the cream swirl into the darkness. "We'd dated for two years in high school. It was stupid," she said with a small laugh. "We thought we knew everything. Thought we were really in love. We got careless."

She dumped more sugar in. She couldn't look at him. She didn't want to see whatever expression he was wearing. And it had been a long time since she'd talked about it. Most of the time she forgot it had ever existed . . . he'd ever existed. She had to, to survive. Every once in a while, when she noticed Emily observing fathers at the hospital, it would gnaw at the very core of her soul, condemning her, shaming her. Maybe she should've tried harder to keep him from leaving, but in her heart, she knew that he didn't love her and didn't want a life with her.

"So when I found out I was pregnant, he was getting ready to leave for college and, uh, didn't want anything to get in his way." She found the courage to look at Jason. He looked like he understood, but she couldn't be sure which side he understood more.

She sipped her coffee and gathered a little strength. "But Emily, she's . . . she's the best decision I ever made."

He smiled. And Alexia found herself smiling too.

"So," she said, leaning toward him, "apparently someone came by and covered my back rent. Was it you?"

Jason just shrugged.

"Thank you."

"So I have a question for you, and I hope I'm not being too out of line here."

Well, that wasn't a stretch, but she kept quiet.

"I was wondering if you'd like to join me for Thanksgiving."

Alexia's mouth opened in surprise. Had he just invited her for *Thanksgiving* dinner? She laughed, causing him to blush and look a little regretful, but she couldn't help it. She couldn't even remember the last time she'd been on a date or even been asked out. Was he asking her out? To Thanksgiving dinner? This was bizarre.

"Oh . . . um . . . thanks. That's nice of you to ask, but I can't. Obviously Emily needs me here, so . . . but thanks."

He didn't look the least bit deterred, and the smile turned into a confident grin. "That's too bad, because you're missing out on a splendid example of a way-too-wealthy dysfunctional American family."

Alexia laughed. "You know, I have the strangest feeling I might have enjoyed it."

○ ◇ ○

Emily liked to rub the top of her head. It was smooth. Her mom had bought her some special lotion that smelled like strawberries. She kind of thought hair was overrated these days anyway. You had to brush it and wash it, it got into ketchup and stuff if you weren't careful, and it always hung in your eyes when you were trying to do something important.

But she liked her mom's hair. Sometimes, in the right light, it looked perfectly golden. She liked playing with it sometimes, combing her fingers through it.

Her mother had a book beside her and was looking down at it, but by the way her eyes *weren't* moving back and forth, Emily knew she wasn't reading.

Daydreaming. Emily used to get in trouble for that. She used to get in trouble for a lot of things. She didn't get in trouble anymore, and that's how she knew that the news was getting worse. She could hang from the ceiling and break every valuable thing in the hospital and nobody would say a word.

"What are you thinking about?"

Her mom looked up, wearing the same expression Emily used to wear when she felt the urge to take Sharpies to the walls. There was something about the word *permanent* that made her smile.

Her mother recovered, putting that annoyingly reassuring expression on her face. "Nothin'."

"You're thinking about Jason."

"Yeah. He's weird," her mother said, moving to the bed, "isn't he?"

"He's a good weird."

Her mom closed the book she wasn't reading. "You know, uh, he invited me over to Thanksgiving with his family."

"Oh, really?"

"Of course I told him, 'Whatever, loser.'"

Yeah, right. "I think you should go," Emily said.

"Absolutely not. I wouldn't dream of missing Thanksgiving with you."

That was the problem with her mom these days. She'd stopped dreaming.

○ ◇ ○

Emily watched from her window as she stroked the curtains next to her. There she was, walking down the sidewalk. Emily had helped her pick out what to wear. She was really clueless about fashion. And makeup? Forget about it. She wasn't trying to be rude, but finally she'd had to explain to her mom that without a little blush, she was going to look awfully pale.

Belinda watched out the window with her. "Mission accomplished."

"Two completely opposite people who wouldn't have had a chance without me." She glanced at Belinda. "Destined to make each other miserable."

"Well, aren't you the romantic?"

"Just practical."

Belinda tickled her ribs. "Oh, come on now. I see how you look at Michael down the hall."

Emily folded her arms and watched Belinda return to messing with the monitors. "He's gross. He's disgusting. He picks his nose."

"Don't worry. They all pick their noses. It's just what men do. They also breathe fire and smell like garbage."

Emily laughed. "Plus, I can beat him at Jenga, which is just pathetic."

"Get used to it, girl. You'll always be smarter than the boys."

Emily smiled and turned back to watch her mom. She was waiting down below with Jason at the bus stop. "Think they'll have a good time?"

"As good a time as any woman can have with a stinky boy."

"He better not mess up, or I swear I'll give him a black eye he won't forget."

◊ ◊ ◊

Alexia had forgotten how awkward dates could be. Or whatever this was. She certainly had never gone on a date to celebrate a major American holiday, that was for sure. *Stop fussing with your scarf,* she told herself. *You're going to look nervous.*

She was nervous. One, she was on a date. Two, she was on a date with a guy who just days ago had actually been a bum. Three, something told her as dysfunctional as *he* seemed, his family might put *his* dysfunction to shame.

As they waited for the bus, Jason turned to her, his hands clasped in front of him like a perfect gentleman. "So why did you decide to come?"

"My daughter banished me."

He smiled. "So I have you by decree?"

"Knowing Emily, by design."

She could smell the fumes from the bus long before it rounded the corner. It rumbled toward them and Jason stepped back from the curb a little. The bus doors swooshed open, and Alexia stepped on. But as she turned to go to the back of the bus, she noticed Jason wasn't coming.

What now? Could this guy be any more high maintenance? Had he changed his mind?

She glanced down at her scarf. Maybe it was the scarf. Maybe she should've left the scarf off. She'd told Emily she shouldn't wear the scarf.

But as she studied Jason, she realized it wasn't regret on his face. It was fear. Actual fear. He was going pale. "You okay, Jason?"

He nodded, but his eyes had a weird glazed look about them.

"Oh, don't tell me you've never been on a bus before." By the way he wasn't moving, it was likely he had never taken any sort of public transportation. She stepped down and grabbed his sleeve. He followed, stared at all the people staring back at him. She took a seat. "Just a little warning. You might have to grab a—"

The bus lunged forward and Jason stumbled backward, nearly knocking the people behind him down like bowling pins. She pointed to the strap he was supposed to be holding. He gave a nervous smile and grabbed on to it.

Ah, the beginning of a Cinderella moment made in public transportation heaven. But, she had to admit, he was growing on her.

chapter 10

The long, exquisite table seemed like something to be found in a castle, not a dining room. Alexia listened to the conversations around her. The family looked familiar with one another but not exactly eager to be together. A strange tension hung over the room, stifling what should have been a festive occasion. Alexia glanced at Jason, who smiled.

A voice suddenly rose over the noise. It was Bill, the man Jason had introduced as his uncle but said nothing more about. "You know," he said, peering around the table, "I had my firm do an informal audit—just the financials of the publicly held side— and there're still several hundred million floating around."

"You knew him better than I," said the other uncle, Jack. "Most of those companies were privately held."

"Maybe we should check into some of his favorite charities? They do have to report large contributions," Bill said, stuffing his mouth full of turkey.

Alexia felt something under her feet. A cat? She glanced down. A kid. A little big to be crawling under the tables, but at least that gave this family a sense of normalcy.

"That's a great idea. You know Daddy was always a sucker for a begging hand."

Bill looked to be contemplating this. He nodded slightly. "Unfortunately, you're right."

The conversation continued, but Alexia's attention was torn away from it by Ruth, Jason's aunt. Her accent said "sweet Southern girl," but something told Alexia she wasn't about to ask for a pie recipe. "And what sort of business does your family come from, Alexia?"

Alexia hesitated, looking at Jason, who assured her through his calm eyes that Ruth was probably harmless. "Um . . . health care."

"Oh, how wonderful!" Ruth exclaimed. Everyone looked in their direction. "We have a wing in the hospital downtown. A couple of wings, I think. Or is it a couple of hospitals? I always forget." She tossed out a careless laugh.

"My daughter is receiving great care thanks to your father."

Ruth's laugh faded into a polite smile.

"Great sector, health care." Bill's voice boomed with authority. "A little flat in the third quarter, but poised to rocket."

Jason took his fork and tapped it against his crystal water glass. He looked determined. "I'd like to propose a toast."

"Yes!" declared Bill as he raised his glass. "To each other, for suffering through a year of . . ." Bill chose his words carefully. ". . . great adjustment."

Mischief twinkled in Jack's eyes. "Excuse me, but does anyone else seem to notice it smells a little like cowhide in here?"

"And how are those sin stocks of yours doing, Jack?" Ruth asked, her southern accent giving way to the snideness in her voice.

Bill grabbed Jack's shoulder and with a wide smile said, "And what's wrong with a little investment in alcohol, tobacco, and firearms?"

"Over the stench of oil," Ruth inserted.

"And what's wrong with oil, thank you very much?" Bill said.

Ruth raised an eyebrow at her brother. "My money's just as green in Manhattan as anywhere else."

"So," Bill said, his gaze scanning the table, "who does get the rest of the estate? Sarah?"

Jason's mother, who had disengaged from the conversation awhile back, snapped upright. "I don't know anything about that." Her puffy lips smiled mildly.

"Well, you were the last one in there," Jack pointed out. The room suddenly grew uncomfortably quiet.

"No, I wasn't," Sarah said definitively, tossing her hair over her shoulder.

Bill's wife—Alexia couldn't remember her name, but she was stunningly beautiful, with dark hair and porcelain skin—spoke up. "Well, that's just ridiculous, darling. When we left, you were the only one there."

Sarah put a gentle hand on Jason's shoulder. "Well, Jason was also there."

Alexia watched Bill's eyes narrow and focus on Jason. "Ah," he said without a hint of warmth. "Jason."

"So," Jack said, "enlighten us, Jason. You certainly could not have been the one to receive the bulk of Red's estate."

"Or are you?" Ruth chimed in.

Bill's voice was full of tempered fury. "Is that why you insisted we get together for Thanksgiving? So you could reveal your newly enhanced trust fund to us?"

Alexia watched Jason, fearful he was about to explode. But instead, he looked very much in control. In a calm voice he said, "It's Thanksgiving. I was hoping maybe we could all go around the table and each say something that we're most thankful for."

Alexia smiled. She couldn't think of anything better—

Suddenly the room exploded with laughter, and it wasn't the nice kind.

"Are you on crack, Jason?" Jack roared.

"Again?" Ruth chortled.

"Well," Jack said, raising his glass to Bill, "here's a thanks: we don't have to put up with Dad's endless litany of cliché quotes this season."

"Or hand-spun, cornpone wisdom," Bill mocked.

"Here, here!" someone said from the end of the table. Everyone turned and looked at Sarah's grinning boyfriend, who immediately stopped grinning.

"Who is that?" Bill asked quietly.

"I think he works down at the video store," Jack replied.

Alexia laughed to herself. Jason was right. This dysfunction went deep. She glanced up to find Jack's attention on her, his eyes less than friendly.

"Well, Jason will tell you all you need to know about this man, this dearly departed," Jack said, his eyes shifting to Jason. "I mean, he, more than anyone here, has a bone to pick with the late, great Red Stevens."

Jason only looked at his plate, apparently trying to restrain himself.

Suddenly a voice broke through the tension. "Jason, I can only imagine what you've just been through . . ."

Someone gasped. Someone else asked, "Is that . . . Red?"

The voice sounded like it was coming from a television or a radio. "I could never get them to be thankful for anything, either. But I have a good idea that along the way you'll realize what it means to be family."

"What in the world is that?" Bill asked, glancing up at the ceiling like he expected something to be hovering there.

Everyone started murmuring. Then Jason leaped suddenly from the table, rushing over to the small kids' table in the corner of the room.

"Give me that!" he barked to one boy, but the kid tossed whatever it was across the table to another kid, who tossed it again as Jason tried to grab it.

The voice continued. "Jason, if you do succeed, you'll be one step closer to all I have for you."

Jason finally snatched it back. It looked like a small toy or a GameBoy.

"What's 'all I have for you'?" Jack asked, his face beginning to glow with anger.

"It's between him and me," Jason said. "It's none of your business."

"It has everything to do with us!" Bill shouted. "It's our money!"

Alexia watched Jack try to settle his brother down before he turned back to Jason. "So," he said smoothly, "he's making you work for your inheritance?"

"Not anymore," Jason replied, "because I don't think I could ever win at this one. Alexia, let's go."

Alexia quickly rose, her napkin dropping to the table. She could feel herself trembling as she followed Jason out into the marble foyer, where their footsteps echoed off the wall.

"Jason!" his mother called after him. "Wait. Wait!"

"Don't," he said as he stopped and turned, glaring at her.

"Honey," she said, "just tell them what they want to hear."

"I don't have to tell them anything."

Alexia moved closer to Jason as Bill made his way out. "Jason, you're gonna hear from my attorney Monday morning."

"Ditto," said Jack from behind him.

"Shut up, Jack," Bill said.

Alexia watched Jason make eye contact with each of them, fully taking in their attempt to look like a force to be reckoned with.

"You're pathetic," Jason said, then turned and walked through the enormous front doors. Alexia nearly had to run to keep up with him.

"Wait. Jason, slow down!"

He didn't. Instead, he gestured toward the house. "I put up with that for years! I was a part of that."

Alexia had nearly caught up with him. "What happened to your dad?" she asked breathlessly.

"He's dead. What else do you want to know?"

"How'd he die?"

"The only person who really knows just took it to his grave."

◇ ◇ ◇

Alexia trailed Jason down the aisle of the bus, hanging on to the loops for balance.

"Jason," she said as he plopped himself down into a seat. She looked at him with gentle eyes, trying to convey what maybe her words couldn't. "There's something I always want you to remember. When I met you, you were a . . ." She smiled a little as she took the seat in front of him. "A homeless person. You made friends with my daughter. We shared peanut butter and jelly sandwiches. All this without me knowing anything about your background."

He sighed heavily. "Yeah, well, the problem is that's me back there."

"Yeah, but you can walk away from all that." Alexia felt the words prick her own heart. What she wouldn't give to be able to walk away from the "all that" of her life. Just take Emily and go.

Start walking and never stop. She smiled at him. "You already have."

"Look, I appreciate what you're saying, but money changes things. It gets you stuff. It's a way to live life worry free. Money takes away the worry."

"Yeah, I saw what money can do." Alexia heard the harshness in her own voice, but she didn't care. "And your worries, or whatever you want to call them—they're not life or death, Jason."

"Okay, I'm sorry. But my getting this inheritance is a matter of life or death, and I know when I say that I sound like I'm being a Stevens, and being a Stevens is all about money. But it's not. It's more."

He seemed to transform right in front of her. Moments before he'd been a man who wanted to toast the blessings in his life. Now he looked consumed by what he didn't have and what now looked to be out of his reach. Alexia turned from him, and they didn't speak for the rest of the bus ride.

How could she have let herself get tangled up with him? She knew better! She had known men like him her whole life. Why hadn't she kept her guard up and written him off to be just like the others?

The bus stopped in front of the hospital, and Alexia didn't wait to see if he was coming. She de-boarded the bus and walked toward the front doors without looking back. But soon enough he was beside her again. Wordlessly they strolled as Alexia tried to get a grip on her emotions before going back in. She didn't want Emily to see disappointment in her face. Her little girl had wanted her to have a good time, and that's what she was going to see—that Alexia had had the time of her life.

"So, I'll pay you back as soon as possible," she said abruptly.

Jason stopped walking as she continued on. "What?" he asked.

"The money I owe you. The sixteen hundred."

Jason just stared at her.

"Happy Thanksgiving," she said.

◇ ◇ ◇

"Jason."

"Hamilton. Can I come in?" Jason looked at his shoes. "I know it's late."

Hamilton opened the door wider. "I thought you might come by today."

Jason gave him a curious look but walked in. He stood in the foyer a moment and glanced around, but his mind seemed to be far away.

"Come into my study."

Jason followed Hamilton. He wasn't saying much, which was a first. That kid usually didn't know when to shut up. Hamilton went to the wet bar and poured a snifter of cognac. He watched Jason make his way around the room until he stopped at the mantel. He stood considered thoughtfully as he contemplated the photograph on top. Hamilton smiled to himself. It was a small victory, but getting the kid to be quiet and think was a step in the right direction nonetheless.

"Marietta Ruby," Hamilton said, approaching Jason from behind. Handing him the cognac, he studied the picture, as he did every single morning. He never got tired of looking at it and his heart never stopped hurting when he did. "From the time I met her in the seventh grade, that was my sweetheart."

Jason studied the photograph more intently.

"She didn't make it easy, though. Took me all the way till the eighth grade to catch up with her."

Jason smiled. "She's beautiful."

"Yeah. She passed away shortly after we were married." Hamilton could barely get the words out. It still seemed impossible that she was gone.

"I'm really sorry." The kid looked it too. Huh.

"The greatest gift she gave me was the will to move on, to overcome."

"You know," Jason said, "I may have met someone myself."

Hamilton stared at the photo in front of them. "Then cherish her. And become the man she deserves."

For a moment the two men stood in silence. Then Hamilton gestured toward a chair. "Have a seat."

Jason did, cupping his cognac as he got comfortable.

"Now, as I said, I had a feeling you were going to stop by."

Hamilton reached for the remote. Dread filled his expression, but he kept silent, so Hamilton switched on the video. Jason turned toward it and looked resigned to taking in whatever Red was going to say.

"That university you attended, what was it rated? Number

three? Number three party school in the country."

Jason cut his eyes sideways. Hamilton could only shrug. Red had a way with words.

"Do you truly know how to learn?" Red continued. "Jason, any process worth going through will get tougher before it gets easier. That's what makes learning a gift. Even if pain is your teacher."

At the word *pain*, Jason flinched, then stared with steely eyes at the envelope Hamilton handed him. It was almost as if he knew what was coming next, but he reached out and took it anyway. Opening it, he carefully pulled out the papers. He drew in a breath as if to prepare himself. When he opened the papers, his eyes grew wide. He stood.

"No! There's no way. Anywhere but there." He threw the papers on the table and headed for the door, then turned back to Hamilton. "I know what he's trying to do, and it's not gonna work. He can take his millions to his grave. I don't care."

"What he's trying to do is for your benefit, Jason, not your destruction."

"You know, Hamilton, you sound just like him. But guess what. You're not him."

"I don't know, son," Hamilton said. "I do have one of his kidneys."

chapter 11

emily watched Jason from her hospital room, where she and her mom peered down below. He'd been walking around and around and around that stupid fountain for what seemed like forever.

"He's been out there for hours," Emily said with a long sigh.

"Yep. He's got some big decisions to make," her mother replied.

Emily knew her mom stayed neutral for her sake. She'd learned a long time ago about staying neutral. That's what all of her doctors did. They wouldn't say yes and they wouldn't say no. They would just stay right in the middle. She hated that. She would rather they just tell her it was over and be done with it. Or tell her all this stupid chemotherapy was going to do something other than make her hair fall out. She wished they would tell it like it was. Just once.

"Do you think he'll come in or go home?" Emily asked.

Her mother tried a smile. "He doesn't have a home."

Well, that was one way to get out of answering the question. Emily turned and grabbed her coat and umbrella.

"Hey, what are you doing?"

Emily walked out of her room. She could hear her mother hurrying behind her.

"Emily! Stop! Wait! What are you doing?"

Emily arrived at the elevator and pushed the down arrow. To her delight, it dinged and the doors opened. She stepped in while her mother scrambled to catch up.

"Emily, listen to me." Her mother tried her calm voice, the one she used when she was getting upset but didn't want to show it because Emily was sick and mothers of sick children don't yell at them, no matter what they've done. That was one perk in this whole thing: she could get away with just about anything.

Downstairs, the doors swished open, and Emily walked out, but this time her mother grabbed her arm. "Emily, you stop it right now!"

Okay . . . so there *was* a line. Interesting. Emily turned to her mother and put her hands on her hips. "I need to talk to him."

"No, you don't."

"Yes, I do."

"No."

"Yes."

Her mother sighed and stood upright, shaking her head. "Look, Emily, I know there seems like there should be an easy solution to this, but there's not, okay?"

"It all depends on how you look at it."

"Whatever the case, you're not going out there."

Emily tried a different angle. "Mom . . ." she said, her voice going tender. "There are just some things I need to say."

That worked. Her mother's expression softened. "What things?"

Emily lowered her eyes. "He might not ever be back. I want to tell him some things."

Her mother knelt and grabbed her hands. "You just want to say good-bye?"

Emily nodded and pulled her lips down into a sad smile. "Yeah. That."

Her mother rose and looked to be contemplating this. "Okay, well, I'm going with you."

"No. I need to do this on my own. You can stay here by the front doors. You can see me."

"But I—"

"You don't even have your coat. And the rule is that you have to have your coat to go outside." Ha. That was a good one. Using one of her silly rules against her.

"Fine." Her mother gestured toward the door. "But make it quick, okay? Are you sure you're going to be all right? I don't want you to get upset."

"I'll be fine." Emily smiled, then turned and walked out the front door. Putting the umbrella over her head, she marched straight toward Jason. Before she was even close, she knew he could hear her boots coming. They were coming to do some serious stomping.

"You're right," she said. Jason stopped and turned to her. "She hates you."

"I know." He looked as pathetic as he sounded.

"Then why are you here?"

Jason searched for words. "I have to leave the country for a while. I'm reluctant to go because of what I'm leaving behind."

"What are you leaving behind?"

The idiot just stood there. He had his chance and he was just standing there like a stupid person. Her mother might be good at controlling her temper, but Emily was not. In a quivering voice she said, "Then you have to go. Now get out of here!"

Jason looked surprised, but he stepped off the fountain and started walking toward the street. The weakling! He couldn't even stand up to her? Fight for what he wanted? "You screwed up big time, you know!" she shouted at him. "I had to eat rubbery hospital turkey for Thanksgiving!"

Emily turned to walk back to the hospital, but she wasn't done yet. "You better be back by Christmas!" she yelled at him. And this time she didn't look back. She didn't want to see him go. She didn't want to see him not turn around. She only wanted to see her mother, who was standing at the glass door looking worried as usual.

"Are you okay?" her mother asked anxiously.

Emily put on her own smile. "I feel much better."

○ ◇ ○

Holding a small duffel bag, Jason stood just outside the security gates of the airport, watching the people pass him by, clutching their boarding passes and driver's licenses, hurrying around one another like their business might be the only important thing around.

He, too, was clutching a boarding pass and a driver's license, but he wasn't moving. He couldn't move. It was like his feet were glued to the tile.

What was moving was his mind, which hadn't stopped since Hamilton had given him the envelope. *It's for your benefit, not your destruction.* Still, it didn't make sense. He couldn't fathom how this, of all things, would be beneficial. This seemed cruel, and it was something he'd always suspected of his grandfather—that he had a cruel side.

So why was he here? What had made him get out of bed this morning, pack his bags with what little he had, and stand here like he might actually go?

An old woman with the airline emblem stitched to her polyester jacket came up beside him. "Sir, how can I help you?" Jason looked down at her. As far as he could remember, nobody had ever offered to help him at an airport, and usually when he needed help, nobody was around. "You look lost," she added, just in case he might be confused about why she was asking.

"No. I'm not lost."

"Are you found?" She smiled at her own joke. "I'm just kidding. I have a sense of humor. A lot of people don't like it. It's just that *lost* and *found* go so well together, don't they? Maybe it's because I used to work in lost-and-found, and boy, what a job that was. You couldn't imagine the things people leave behind and the—"

"Look," Jason said, holding up a polite hand, "I appreciate it, but I'm not lost. Or found. I'm thinking."

She looked toward the security line. "Don't let it intimidate you. It moves faster than you'd think. And I know those people get to hollerin' about taking your shoes and belts off and your laptops out, but they're just trying to get people through. It's not personal."

"I'm not worried about security. Don't I have a right to stand here and think?"

"I suppose you do. People need to do more thinking, in my opinion." She paused. "What are you thinking about?"

"Ma'am," Jason said, his patience sliding off him by the second, "it's personal, okay? It's nothing that I want to discuss or could even explain to someone I know, much less a stranger."

"Well, dear, that's understandable. Is it a girlfriend?"

Jason looked away. "It's a lot of things. Now, isn't there a little kid wandering around without his mother that you need to help?"

"I tell you, what I wouldn't have given for this kind of transportation back in my day. My Joseph and me, we were an ocean apart, and mail took forever to get back and forth. Nowadays I could just get on an airplane and be halfway around the world. Nothing would've kept me apart from him. I would've gone."

"I'm not going to see a girlfriend."

"Well," she said, patting him on the arm, "I don't know what it is, but it means a great deal to you." She nodded toward the security line. "Go on. Don't waste another minute. And don't worry. Nobody's going to be staring at the holes in your socks."

chapter 12

Jason's fingers gripped his seat as the topless Jeep that wouldn't know a shock absorber if it bumped into one bumbled along one dirt road after another. It seemed they'd been driving for hours. Now *this* was an off-road adventure that the off-road vehicle he'd bought last year couldn't touch. Not that he would know. He'd never driven it off road.

Earlier, from the prop plane, he'd seen the jungle, which stretched far and wide and out of his view. It was lush and green, expansive like it was its own continent. The air smelled fresh, felt thick.

They'd come in for a hard landing on a dirt runway that didn't look long enough for a car to stop on it. And now he was on the way to some village. By the looks of the paths they were taking, it was deep inside this beautiful and terrifying jungle.

They finally rounded a bend, splashed through a small creek that drenched him, and came to a dusty halt in front of wooden buildings that didn't look like they could withstand a slight breeze.

If Jason hadn't been so ready to ditch the Jeep, he might've liked to stay in it. Instead, he found his boot touching the earth of this foreign place. He glanced around, noticing an ominous mountain looming in the distance. Something told him it was that mountain. Many rose from the earth, but that one seemed to call his name. Then he noticed a large wooden sign: "Stevens Biblioteca." Jason shook his head. "Even down here, you put your name on everything." Red's ghost knew how to haunt a guy.

The locals started gathering, some looking with pure curiosity, others smiling and nodding like they'd known him for years. Men immediately began unloading the crates of books in the back of the Jeep, and before he knew it, someone had taken his hand. A small woman with a large smile gazed at him wide eyed, as if she'd seen some sort of astronomical phenomenon. "Welcome. Oh, welcome!" she said in a thick accent. "Jason Stevens." She said his name with more affection than anyone he'd ever met, including his family. And without hesitation she pulled him into a tight hug. "Oh!" she gasped and studied him with her hand on her heart. "So good to meet you. I am Bella."

"Hi." Jason managed.

Her face lit with excitement. "May I be the first to show you inside the library your grandfather built?"

A reluctance made him pause, but it didn't look like Bella would take no for an answer. "Yeah. Sure."

"Good, good." She pulled him forward, opened the door, and gestured for him to enter. She trailed him in, right on his heels, her smile eagerly anticipating his reaction. Jason wanted to be polite, but this wasn't what he'd expected. The floor was covered in dirt, the shelves nearly empty. The books that were there looked several decades old.

"Where are all the books?"

Bella glanced around inquisitively. "Ah, you joke."

Jason raised an eyebrow. He was beginning to think the joke was on him.

"With the people. Is it not like that in the great libraries in los Estados Unidos?"

Jason didn't answer. It might be a trick question. Bella hovered near him as she gestured toward the shelves. "Villagers wait for books. You bring them new books, and they are waiting for you to pick up old books. Exchange. Library. Sí?"

Sí. He ran his finger along an empty shelf. Dust clung to the air and shimmered in the sunlight let in from a crack in the wooden roof. He picked up a thick book, and the binding nearly ripped off as he held it. "So basically I'm in a third-world country at a backwoods library with no books, and the books that are here I can't even read." He snapped the book shut. "Great."

Bella looked undaunted, but Jason suspected nothing was

lost in translation. With a knowing look, she made her way over to an old desk, pulled out a drawer, and slipped her hand inside. Turning, she put an envelope up to her chest, clutching it as her warm eyes locked with his. "This I found when I was cleaning his desk . . . once I heard of Red's passing." She handed it to him.

The envelope was addressed to his grandfather in the writing of a ten-year-old boy. Jason's handwriting. "Thought maybe you would like to keep?" The sadness of Bella's tone faded, and the twinkle returned to her eyes. "When you sent this to him, he proudly showed it to all of us."

He remembered everything about the day he'd written this.

"Then the tragedy. Broke his heart."

Jason folded the envelope and stuck it in his back pocket. "Listen," he said in carefully pronounced English. "I'm tired. Tired?"

"Sí, sí." She guided him out the door. "You need rest, no?"

"Sí. Yes."

"We have kept the nicest bed for you."

○ ◇ ○

As if the Jeep ride hadn't tortured his body enough, the bed was now doing a fine job of keeping him awake. He just wanted to sleep a little, but sleeping on plywood wasn't what he'd had in mind. There was a pillow, but it smelled musty. Still, it was a place to lay his head and do what he'd been doing a lot of lately.

112

Thinking. What he wouldn't give for a stupid, mind-numbing video game, pool game, card game. Anything but this.

He closed his eyes, trying to remember what his old life had been like. How amazing that one man's journey off the earth could cause so much trouble for someone still on it. He'd been perfectly content. Then, seemingly overnight, his life was disrupted in a way he never would've been able to fathom, a barely flickering flame fighting a fierce wind.

He tried to keep his eyes closed, tried to force out all the memories that were beating on the doors of his mind. But he couldn't. Whether his eyes were open or closed, all he could see was himself, ten years old, sitting at his desk in his room, where he'd begun spending more and more time.

Sighing, he opened the letter. He first studied the bubbly handwriting, remembering when he'd decided to make it slant more like his father's handwriting, hoping it seemed more mature.

Dear Grandpa,
How's Ecuador? I miss you and Dad so much.

Tears rushed to his eyes, and he squeezed them shut. It was like he was ten again, his heart an open wound. He'd driven his mother and every other relative crazy asking when his father would be back. He remembered putting so much thought into the letter, carefully constructing it so his grandfather would know how serious he was.

You know my birthday is coming up, and I was thinking, instead of giving me gifts this year, could you take me on one of your trips? I promise I won't cause any trouble.

Jason smiled a little. That came from the I-can't-take-you-any-where line his mother was always throwing at him. He did cause her a lot of trouble, but then again, she did the same for him.

I just want to see you and dad again soon. Write back please.
Love, Jason

Jason lowered the letter, and as he did, the mountain came into full view from the small window, swallowing up its space. Everywhere he looked, there it was, and Jason couldn't take his eyes off it.

He carefully folded the letter and stuffed it into his bag. Turning onto his back, he stared up at the wooden ceiling. It had been years since he'd allowed himself to think of his dad. Or his grandfather.

His eyes, heavy as they closed, saw his grandfather walking into his home, clutching a box. Jason had skipped three stairs at a time to greet him. But his grandfather hadn't hugged him or even smiled.

Instead, he'd knelt down right there in front of the door, set the box down, and squeezed both of Jason's forearms. He stared at the floor.

"Grandpa?" Jason had asked. "What's wrong?"

He could hear his mother crying in another room, and later he found out that she couldn't bear to tell him, so she'd made Red come over and do it.

He never actually said it. But he cried and apologized and cried some more, then told Jason he needed to be strong. Even at ten, Jason wondered how he could be strong when his own grandfather was crying at his feet. He knew it was a plane crash, but that was all he was told. It was a few months later at a family dinner when Jason had found his grandfather in his study alone, staring out a dark window.

"Grandpa?"

He'd turned around. Before the crash, he would've opened his arms and invited Jason over. But with every day that went by, it seemed his grandfather changed more and more.

"What is it?"

"I want to know about Dad."

His grandfather's eyes barely registered he'd been spoken to.

"Grandpa?"

"There's nothing to say."

Jason stepped forward toward a man who used to make him feel at ease. He clasped his shaking hands behind his back. It had taken him twenty minutes to get up the courage to talk to him. "I want to know what happened."

"You know what happened. Why do you want to know more? What good thing could come of it?"

"Why won't you tell me?" Jason's voice quivered.

He watched his grandfather stare at the ground, his eyes

distant and sad, his lips pressed together in a hard, straight line. "You need to leave this alone."

"You're not telling me everything!" Jason's fists were now at his side, balled up, while his face turned hot.

"You listen to me," his grandfather said, his tone low but curt in just the right way to make Jason fear everything about him. "Your father was a good man. He was trying to get to villagers. Sometimes bad things happen. Okay?" His grandfather's voice choked in barely audible emotion. "There is nothing more to say."

But Jason had a lot more to say. At ten, though, he knew it could be summed up in three words. "I hate you."

And from that day on, that man had never been "Grandpa" again. He became "Red."

chapter 13

Jason had awoken early. The sun, barely peeking over the tops of the trees, kept watch over the quiet village. He rose and walked the short path to the library. He was beginning to appreciate the pleasantness of this time of morning. He spent the first part of the morning repairing the damaged books. He glued the spines back on, making sure the pages were level and the books still opened with ease. Then he took a good hour and a half reacquainting himself with the Dewey Decimal System. He remembered his school librarian lecturing on the importance of the stupid thing. Laughing to himself, he recalled his exact words to her: "Once I leave school, I'll never set foot in a library again."

"Is that so?" she asked with measured patience. "Won't you read books?"

He smirked at her. "Of course. But I'll *buy* them."

Jason looked down at the heavy book in his hand, trying to remember the last time he'd actually picked up a book to read. After his father had died, he'd become a voracious reader, immersing himself in worlds where things turned out okay in the end. But after he left college, books became a thing of the past.

His finger rubbed the spine of the book he was holding. Maybe he was still waiting for his happy ending.

Shaking off the memories that continued to swarm him like gnats, he sat down at the simple wooden desk where he'd been working. The book he held had been damaged by what looked like sun and water. The pages were warped and the spine bent nearly in half. His hands moved over all of it. The smell was sour, and mold dotted the paper.

This is me.

It's what he felt like, anyway—an old, used book, insignificant with all its damage.

Behind him, Jason heard someone walk in. People had been coming and going all day.

"*Un momento, por favor,*" Jason said.

"You look just like your father."

Jason froze, lifting his eyes, gaining the nerve to turn around. He set the book down carefully and turned to find a man leaning against one of the bookcases. He wore a dark felt hat and a blue shirt jacket. His expression gave nothing away.

"I was here the night he died."

"It happened up on that mountain, didn't it?" The man simply stood there. "Take me there?"

"You cannot go. It is now the province of the drug lords."

Jason stood, his words impulsive. "You don't understand. I'll pay you." He paused. "Well, someday."

"I understand you perfectly," the man said calmly. "But, señor, I only have one life."

"You're just bargaining now, aren't you?"

"Señor Stevens, you do not want to pay the price it would take." The man's words held a dire warning. "No one who goes there returns."

Suddenly a noise erupted outside, jolting Jason. Drums thumped and wooden instruments whistled festive melodies. A girl appeared in the doorway.

"Is time!" she said excitedly. *"Venga!"*

Jason was ushered outside, pulled by his arms into a crowd of revelry. He glanced back, trying to find the stranger, but he'd vanished.

Absorbing the emotion of it all, Jason allowed himself to be pulled into a tent, where everyone sat in a large circle. Their eager smiles urged him in. Bella gestured grandly. "Our guest of honor! Mr. Jason Stevens!"

The noise grew louder as they greeted him with claps and shouts and all forms of affection. Jason felt a little silly, but then again, he couldn't remember the last time anyone had made him feel this appreciated. He still wasn't sure what he was being appreciated for, but it was in his nature to always enjoy a party.

Bella put a headdress of brightly colored feathers on his head, then took his hand and led him to what Jason could only guess was a privileged spot for the feast. "Sit, sit," she said enthusiastically as the tribal music continued to beat all around him.

"Um . . . okay . . ." Jason had just sat down when women began bringing food to him. Hardly a thing on the plate was recognizable, and although he hated caviar, he thought he'd rather eat bucket loads of it rather than whatever it was he was getting ready to consume—which, oddly, looked as though it might've been killed just a few minutes ago.

"Uh . . ." Jason began. "I'm afraid to ask . . ."

"Oh, you will love it!" Bella assured him. "It's so rare that we catch one!"

"Oh . . ."

Suddenly, to Jason's surprise, the music stopped, and for a moment he thought it was because he wasn't gobbling up the contents on his plate. Then Bella leaned over and told him, "The chief is going to talk."

"Estamos aquí para celebrar los que mantienen viva la biblioteca commemorativa de Señor Jay Stevens," the chief said, smiling.

As the crowd cheered, Bella turned to Jason and explained, "He says we are here to celebrate you and those who keep the Jay Stevens Library alive."

"Oh no . . . no, no. He must be mistaken," Jason said, looking at Bella. "My grandfather was very generous. Everything's named after him."

Bella shook her head. "No. It is the Jay Stevens Memorial Library."

Jason wasn't sure which emotions were bursting through him, but they were good. They felt good. Real. He smiled at the chief and then at Bella, who seemed pleased by it all.

"*Usted es huésped honorado,*" the chief said.

Jason watched as they began sipping their drinks. *Here it goes.* He gulped a drink that sent a warm sensation all the way through his body. Smiling, he raised his glass back to the leader and nodded his approval. "To my father."

"*Salud! Salud!*" the chief responded. Then he gestured for a woman to get Jason another drink.

Before he knew it, the room was spinning in the most amazing way. Was he floating? Was someone carrying him? Every time he closed his eyes, it felt like he slept. And for the life of him, he couldn't stop grinning.

Then he spotted him, over near the door to the tent, wearing that same hat and shirt jacket, staring at him as if he could see his soul. And, like before, the mysterious stranger vanished.

◇ ◇ ◇

The festivities had apparently died down, and Jason found himself comfortably napping on a cot. How he'd gotten there, he didn't know, but his mind wasn't as muddled now, and he was able to stand to his feet. Nobody seemed to be around. Was it morning? He couldn't be sure, but there was daylight.

He stumbled forward, trying to get his bearings. Then he spotted it. The Jeep sat right in front of the library. In the distance, the mountain loomed, coming in and out of focus. Jason felt like he could sleep for another three days, but instead he climbed into the Jeep. It started with a roar and, pushing the clutch in, he sped away from the village, splashing through a tiny creek. Nothing was going to stop him. He had to get to that mountain. Even if it meant it would cost him his life.

"You cannot hope to find it without me."

Jason was startled and turned to find the stranger who had haunted him even in his dreams climbing out from underneath the tarp in the backseat. Jason smiled a little and got as comfortable as he could in his seat. "How'd you know I'd go?"

The man's eyes twinkled. "You are a Stevens, are you not?"

"I thought you said you couldn't take me."

"My purpose in coming to you is a promise I made to Señor Red, that you could learn the truth."

Jason remained silent, staring forward.

"He had one desire and one desire alone," the man continued. "To ask your forgiveness. He said one day you would come. Only then could you learn the truth."

They drove in silence for a while, the Jeep climbing the dirt path of the jungle, sometimes struggling up the steeper hills. They'd rounded some dense brush when the man said, "Stop the Jeep."

Jason shoved down on the brake, and dust rose from behind. They both jerked forward, and then the Jeep came to a complete stop. They climbed out of the vehicle, and the man pointed Jason toward a small opening in the tangled mess of the jungle. Without a word, both men stepped into the thick jungle foliage, ducking under limbs and stepping over emerald-colored vines as thick as trees. The sounds of birds and animals swelled like a chorus. Above them, Jason caught glimpses of the kind of shining sky that made one stop and breathe and take time to look up.

They rounded more dense brush, and then Jason saw it. It seemed so small, much smaller than Jason had ever imagined. One wing was broken and bent upward, contorted like a body that had jumped to its death. Trees and bushes and vines cradled the plane.

The man stayed distant, clasping his hands in front of him and bowing his head in respect. Jason walked forward, trembling at the reality of it all. His hands glided over a wing, and then over the door that looked to be jammed shut. The front window was shattered but still intact. The side window, however, had been busted out, with the exception of one shard. Fifteen years of vegetation had grown over it, holding it like a gnarled hand.

Jason leaned inside, emotion catching up with him. He touched the instruments, the yoke, everything he could. He pictured his father flying high in these beautiful skies, above the clouds, enjoying the beauty of it all. He'd loved that about his father. He was able to take life and love it and live it.

But just as quickly as they came, the images faded, and as he backed his head out of the window, he saw his father slumped forward, his head bloody, his limbs twisted, his eyes wide with the fear of knowing death had arrived for him.

Jason tried to hold back the emotion, but he couldn't. Here he was at the very place that had taken his father. He glanced back at the stranger, who stood silently watching. "He had learned of a village . . ." Jason began, his voice cracking. ". . . in the next valley that had a plague and needed medical supplies. But he never understood why Red forbid him to go."

"There was no plague. There was no village."

"What?"

"Red wanted to introduce your father to the oil business. But your father was restless, bored."

Jason shook his head. "No. No!"

"He snuck away. He ran away and took a plane he had no business taking."

"No!" Jason felt as though he'd been struck in the stomach. He couldn't breathe. He couldn't think. He couldn't talk. He could barely stand as he looked up at the man. For the first time, he saw emotion in his eyes. Compassion.

"This is what Red wanted to protect you from. Until now."

Tears dripped down his face. "No."

"There can be no blame for what happened here. The penalty for your father's impulsiveness, unfortunately, was a life. His."

Jason turned away, burying his face in his hands. How could this be? This was why his grandfather had been so distant for so many years? He'd wanted to protect him from the truth? He knew the stranger spoke the truth, because his father had been restless and impulsive. It was what had led him away many times. It was why Jason, as hard as he tried, could never quite catch him.

His sobs turned into deep breaths, and he squeezed his eyes shut. What did it all mean? What was he supposed to do with it?

And then he heard the click of a gun.

chapter 14

A bone-saturating rain drowned out any and all noise. Jason stood by the man who had brought him up here. He didn't even know his name. But in his eyes he saw fear as they stood before a group of men. Bandits. They all had guns and spoke in Spanish. Bella had called them "cocaine cowboys." One of them, the one who seemed to be the leader, looked Jason over. "Americano?"

"He hired me to show him the plane wreck. He likes airplanes."

The bandit stepped closer to them and looked at the man next to Jason. "Up here, my friend, all men are liars." He snatched the man's felt hat and placed it on his own head, then turned and gestured toward the group of men who had huddled

126

around them. "¡Exigimos su rescate! Si nadie los sigue dentro de unas semanas, ¡mátenlos!"

A large man grabbed Jason, turning him and thrusting him forward. Shoved in short spurts, Jason stumbled along. "Wait. Please . . . please . . . don't—" The man pushed him into a small cage. His shoulder slammed against its stone, and before Jason could even stand up, the door was shut and locked.

Jason let his eyes focus in the new darkness. He could see only slices of the rainy sky through the wooden door. A small hole allowed him a peek into the outside world. A few bandits milled around now, but that was it. He wondered where his companion was. He had nothing left. Everything had been taken from him. Crouching with his back against one of the cage walls, he cried, but nothing came out.

All his life he had wanted more. Now all he wanted was his life.

o o o

Jason opened his eyes. All he knew was that it was day. When it rained, he couldn't tell morning from evening. On the days with sun, he could watch through the slits in the cell as the sun passed from one side to the other, but when there were clouds, there was nothing he could do but guess. He wasn't sure how long he'd been asleep. Short periods of sleep didn't give him rest. His body ached from the hard ground, and his mind was in constant motion, trying to find a way out of all of this.

He'd even prayed. He wasn't sure how to pray, but he did it

anyway. Sometimes he would draw pictures in the dirt. Most of the time he sat in the corner, listening to them chatter in a language he couldn't understand, picking up only a few useless words.

Outside he heard commotion. He scrambled to his little hole and peered out with one eye. The men were huddled around something. A couple of them stepped aside, and Jason saw logs piled together. They were trying to start a fire.

It took them no time at all, but the warmth couldn't reach Jason. All he could do was stare at the bright orange flame and try to remember what warmth felt like.

◇ ◇ ◇

"No!" Jason jerked up but realized he'd just been dreaming. He peeked through his hole to see the men carrying something. Boxes. One of them turned a box over and spilled books out onto the fire.

Fuel.

No . . . not the books.

The fire consumed them within seconds, roaring into a blaze that caused the men to gesture like they'd just created a masterpiece. Papers, one by one, swept upward toward the sky then slowly drifted back to the ground.

Jason couldn't watch it anymore. Going back to his corner, he slid downward thinking about Emily, how she'd suffered in pain and lived with the unknown. If he ever saw her again, he'd be better able to look her in the eye. He would understand her more, and maybe she would understand him too.

Suddenly a tin plate slid under the door, pushed by the hand of a man Jason couldn't see. He didn't care. It was food. A piece of bread and a small bowl of beans with no spoon. Some days he got nothing to eat. On those days, he tried to drink the rain when it came.

Snatching the bread, he ripped it apart with his teeth, chewing ferociously and swallowing the pieces nearly whole. He cupped the bowl and drank the beans and soup, all gone in a matter of seconds. He knew he should eat one bite at a time, try to make it last for a few hours. But he was too hungry.

His thoughts carried him back to that awful Thanksgiving when his freaky family decided to show their true colors. He imagined all the food, platefuls, stretching all the way down the table. He'd eaten a few bites. What he wouldn't give for that now. For part of that. For the leftovers off of everyone's plates.

The tears had dried up awhile back, but his heart still hurt. He missed Alexia. She probably thought he'd abandoned her. How would she ever know that he was here, in a cage not fit for an animal, starving to death and going slowly insane?

Would they find his body like they'd found his father's? Would this mountain take both the father and the son?

◊ ◊ ◊

Miss Hastings handed Alexia a tall coffee with cream and then sat down with her at one of the tables in the hospital cafeteria. Alexia tried not to seem anxious. This kind woman had come all the way to the hospital to tell her something, but she was taking her time getting to it.

Finally, she looked at Alexia. "Jason is missing."

"Missing?"

"He went to Ecuador. It was part of this . . . this . . ." Miss Hastings sighed. "The gift."

Alexia shook her head. "I don't understand."

"Jason has been working at a library there, one that was founded by Red and named after Jason's father. It's in a very tiny village."

"Really?" She tried to imagine Jason, who could hardly get himself to ride on public transportation, working in a South American village. But as she looked at Miss Hastings, she could tell something else was wrong. "What's the matter? Can't you find him?"

Miss Hastings's eyes lowered to her coffee. "We think he went searching for the crash site, which is in—" Miss Hastings swallowed "—lawless territory."

"I'm sorry, crash site?"

"Where his father died."

Alexia's fingers wrapped around her coffee as she tried to absorb all of this. So that was what this trip was for. She hadn't really understood why he'd had to leave, but something told her he needed to. At the time, all she could think about was that he was leaving her. But maybe he'd found something—something that might bring him back.

"Is he in any danger?" Alexia asked.

Miss Hastings's eyes glistened, and she looked up apologetically. "I'm so sorry."

○ ○ ○

Combing his fingers through his short beard, he continued to count the strokes. Yesterday he'd made it to 532. He wondered what he looked like with a beard. He'd never grown one. Not even a goatee, when that was the fad.

Food got stuck in it and bugs seemed to think it was their home, so he guarded it any way he could, mostly just with his fingers pulling it. And it proved to be a good distraction from all the thoughts that made him yearn to be dead. He wanted death now. But he couldn't even give himself that. He was stuck, at the mercy of men who hardly regarded him as human but for the small meals given to him when they thought about it.

He'd dreamed last night of Alexia. She was smiling, radiating that warmth that had drawn him to her the first time. Her eyes sparkled with life. But then he'd awoken. Everything was reversed now. When he was awake, that was the nightmare. When he was asleep, that was the reality he wanted to stay in.

Suddenly Jason heard what sounded like paper rattling. He looked out his hole, but he could see no one nearby. Then something caught his eye, above him. It was paper, and it was being slid to him through a crack between the roof and the wall. Jason snatched it and looked at it in the dim light. The writing was in Spanish.

"Fue . . . el mejor . . . y el peor . . . de los tiempos."

A voice came from the other side. "It was the best of times, it was the worst of times. It was the age of wisdom, it was the age of foolishness." Jason smiled through tears. It was his friend. He was still alive and in the adjoining cell.

He handed another paper over, and another. Jason couldn't believe it. These were the pages long missing from the books in the library. Hours went by. Jason read the Spanish on the pages. His companion would translate. He'd never known how hungry he could be for words.

". . . cuanto tiempo o permiso corto al cielo."

"Neither love nor hate thy life; but what thou livest, live well, however long or short may the heavens permit."

Lying on his back, Jason contemplated these words. There was plenty of time to contemplate, and he didn't know how many pages his companion had left, so he didn't want to rush through them. Instead, he took each sentence and thought about it, trying to understand it in every way possible.

Silence guarded the time. Then Jason said, "Tell me about my father."

"In many ways he was very similar to you. Restless. Rebellious. Angry." Jason closed his eyes. The words stung. But he listened anyway. "I think Red saw something in him that he didn't see in his other sons. A fire. The same fire that he saw in you."

Jason rolled over. Everything looked different now. Things

he'd been sure were real were now replaced by the truth. He closed his eyes and fell asleep.

◇ ◇ ◇

In the morning, a loud noise jolted Jason. He leaped to his feet, but the noise was coming from the next cell. "Oh no . . ."

Through the small hole, he could see his companion being dragged off, fighting. The bandits were poking at him, beating him with their guns as he struggled helplessly. A trail of dust was all that remained.

"No . . ." Slumping against the wall, he buried his face in his hands. Every single thing, every small moment of joy, had been taken from him. All he had left was the air he breathed.

chapter 15

t_hump. Thump. Thump._

Jason slowly opened his eyes to the sound. The line between reality and dreams often blurred, so he wasn't sure he was really hearing anything.

Then he heard muffled voices outside. Steps hurrying toward him. He gasped as his cell door flew open. Two arms reached in and pulled him out. Bright sunlight glared hot and white. He barely had time to squint before one of the bandits placed a blindfold over his eyes and secured it tightly behind his head.

Tripping over his own feet, Jason tried to regain his balance. With every step came another hard shove to his back.

"_Amigo?_" Jason tried to raise his voice. "_Amigo?_ Are you here?" He could see nothing, and the voices around him spoke in

Spanish. Was his friend dead?

Then the hands that were shoving him grabbed him by the shoulders, fingers pressing hard into his bones. As he was forced onto his knees, a fear that Jason had never known seized him. He gasped for breath as he listened to rounds being loaded into the chambers of their automatic weapons.

"No, no, no . . . No, no, no, please . . . No!" In his mind flashed pictures of the many hostages he'd seen on the news—blindfolded, hands bound, ready for execution. This was how he was going to die? Executed on the same mountain that had taken his father's life? "I can . . . I can pay you! I have money! Please!" The words left his tongue quickly, too quickly. He had to bargain. But how? What did he have that he could give? "Oh, God, God . . . Does anyone understand what I'm saying?" What Spanish did he know? Not enough to communicate. Maybe he could—

Gunfire. Jason screamed, covering his ears, ducking as though that would help avoid a bullet. More gunfire. Rapid. And more. More. More.

Then silence. Jason waited for the bullet that would take his life.

Suddenly his blindfold was yanked down. Jason stared at the two men on their knees in front of him. Their expressions reflected each other's. No one was dead.

Laughter erupted, and the leader held a bottle of mescal high in the air. *"¡Feliz Navidad!"* he roared, and the others joined in, passing beer around like it was a party. *"¡Feliz Navidad!"* they mocked, jabbing one another with an air of revelry.

Jason couldn't even look at them. Instead, crumpling to the ground, he cried. Pain deeper than he'd ever felt clutched his heart . . . his soul. He was alive. But these men held the power to keep him alive or to kill him. So although he had his life, it wasn't his anymore, to give or to take away. He existed now simply for the pleasure of these cruel and heartless men. His pain was their delight.

And it was Christmas. Wasn't it? He didn't know. What was his family doing? Alexia? Emily?

Slumping forward, Jason managed to lift his eyes, and when he did, he saw him, tied to a tree, his face bloodied, his clothes shredded. Flies swarmed his head. *Amigo.*

Hands grabbed him by the shirt and he was pulled to his feet.

"Vuélvalos a las jaulas! Mañana se mueren!" the leader shouted. Then they pulled Jason up the small hill and drove him back into his cage like an animal. The door slammed, and everything went quiet. Except a sound just outside his door.

Jason looked. The guard was so drunk, he'd forgotten to lock the door.

○ ◇ ○

His mind, as numb as it had become, kept playing their words over in his mind. *Vuélvalos. Las jaulas. Mañana. Mueren.*

What did it mean? The tone had been authoritative, instructive. Several men had looked at Jason and sneered. A few—the younger ones—looked away. He didn't speak their language, but he knew something out of the ordinary had been spoken.

Mueren. Mueren? Muerte . . . Muerte. "Death," he whispered.

Peeking out, Jason tried to see what was happening. A rare stillness covered the camp. The men, passed out from the alcohol, lay scattered around the camp. Their stench clung to the air.

He listened carefully but couldn't identify any sounds indicating anybody was awake or moving around. The bushes and trees made it hard to know for sure. He could see only a few yards. But the man who had been guarding the cells had slid down the wall he usually sat against. The tips of his boots pointed to the sky, and his body lay limp as he slumbered.

Could he escape? He had to escape. This was his only chance. If he ran and got caught, he would surely die. But death was standing nearby anyway.

He pushed the door forward, steadily and slowly. Creeping out, he glanced at the guard. His gun lay nearby, his bottle of beer cradled in his arm.

Jason stepped carefully, trying not to make a sound. He kept himself low, breathed shallowly, watched with alert eyes for anyone who might spot him.

A clearing in the brush looked to be the perfect escape, but where did it lead? Down the mountain or to a cliff?

The time is now.

Stepping over vines and branches, Jason tried not to rush, knowing that would only land him flat on his face. Instead, he watched his steps and hurried through the brush. Limbs scraped his body and he twisted his ankle in a hole, but up ahead he could see a patch of bright sunlight, indicating a clearing.

The brush became less dense, and Jason began jumping over most of it as he headed toward the clearing. He splashed his way through a small creek. The water felt cold and fresh. But he kept running.

And running.

And . . . *amigo.*

Jason slowed, then came to a stop, hardly able to breathe and drenched in sweat. He was free, far from their reach, but his friend was still there. Tied to a tree. Perhaps even being beaten again for Jason's trespass.

Jason looked back toward the steep mountain. He didn't even know the man's name. He hadn't bothered to ask, not once.

It didn't matter. He called him *friend,* and if that's what he was going to call him, then he couldn't leave him.

Jason stepped forward, and with more determination than he'd had going down the mountain, he went back up.

When Jason reached the campsite again, he found all of the bandits passed out except for the man guarding his friend. Amigo, still tied to the tree, looked half dead, with his head leaning against a log and blood dripping down the side of his face.

The guard sat on a crate but seemed to be struggling to stay alert. Jason looked around for anything he could use as a weapon. He noticed a stack of hardbound books sitting nearby.

Grabbing one, Jason approached the guard, who was looking down, focused on lighting a cigar.

You've got one chance. Don't blow it.

He swung the book squarely into the guard's face, knocking him unconscious. Hurrying over to his friend, he shook him, trying to wake him.

"Hey . . . hey . . . hey . . ."

He opened his eyes, looking disoriented. Jason put a finger up. "Shhh."

Jason noticed one of the bandits lying near the fire shift, position, and slap at some mosquitoes on his face, then fall back asleep.

He turned back to his friend. "Can you walk?" he asked, untying the rope that bound his wrists.

His friend managed to sit up a little. "Save yourself!" he whispered.

"Not on your life. Come on." Jason pulled him up and swung an arm around his shoulder, helping him through the brush. Before long, his friend managed to walk without aid, limping and holding his side, but still going. They made it to the creek before they heard the gunfire and shouts in Spanish.

"Hurry," Jason breathed, and they hustled to the clearing, where they broke out into a run.

They ran until dark. Jason could barely walk by the time they sat down near another small stream, cupping their hands to drink. Both reclined against trees, catching their breath. They didn't speak a word. They didn't have to. Both men knew the sacrifice the other had made.

chapter 16

alexia stood with the crowd, staring at the white corridor that should've delivered Jason minutes ago. People had streamed out from customs in droves, but Jason wasn't among them. She watched as couples reunited, mothers held their children, fathers shook hands with their sons. Holding back tears, she made herself stand still and wait. He would be here. She knew it.

And then he appeared, carrying a small black duffel bag. He didn't see her at first. But when he did, his face lit with excitement. Rushing to him, she flung her arms around him and buried her face into his neck.

"What are you doing here?" he asked, holding her tightly.

"I was scared to death." She closed her eyes and blocked out all the fear. Instead, she let this moment saturate every ounce of her. She held nothing back. And neither did Jason. They melted into each other, and the noise of the airport faded. Alexia listened to Jason's breath in her ear.

Finally, Jason released her. "Where's Emily?" he asked.

"Um, she's resting. She'll see you tomorrow."

Jason's eyes brightened as he took her in. "You guys have a good Christmas?"

Alexia tried to hold back the tears. "We didn't have one. How could we?"

"You know what?" he said gently. "We're going to have a fantastic one next year. I promise."

She stepped away from him and looked into his eyes. "We won't have a next year."

○ ○ ○

The concrete, dark and wet, echoed his footsteps against the metal of the long strip of storage units. The security guard's keys rattled next to his hip as Jason walked alongside the man.

"Right up here," the guard said, pointing to a unit on the right. He unlocked it and handed Jason a flashlight. "Lock it back when you're done. Check out with me before you go."

Jason opened the door into blackness. Switching on his light, he guided himself through piles of boxes and other items. This was everything he owned. All crammed into boxes and locked away.

He'd daydreamed about getting his stuff back. Now here it was and he couldn't care less about it.

The light's beam bounced from one item to the next, but Jason was only looking for one thing, and he wasn't going to leave until he found it. Squeezing his body between two towers of boxes, he finally spotted it in the corner. It was piled high with all of his junk, but the drawers were visible, and he reached for the top one and pulled it out. Shirts he hardly ever wore were folded neatly in the drawer. He slipped his hand under one and pulled out a stack of envelopes bound together by a rubber band.

Unopened. Every single one.

He thumbed through them. His first instinct had been to throw them away, but he never could. Instead, he'd hidden them away, like a nasty secret, and they hadn't seen the light of day until now.

He pointed the flashlight toward the first one and tore open the envelope. It was time to hear what his grandfather had to say. This time he would listen.

◇ ◇ ◇

The only noise in the dimly lit conference room was the soft hum of the wall sconces shooting light upward every four feet on the wall. Miss Hastings had been kind enough to let him in and leave him alone. Clutching the letters he'd spent three hours reading and pondering, Jason slowly sat in one of the high-backed leather chairs and turned it to face the video screen.

In letter after letter Red had begged Jason to forgive him, told him of the grief he'd endured, asked for the chance to explain. All tightly sealed away. Jason had never given him that chance. Until now.

A soul-shattering tide of emotion broke through Jason. His grandfather had cared deeply for him and his father. What he could never say in person, he'd bared in ink. He'd spilled out his soul on those pages, and now he was gone. The finality of it all crushed Jason's heart.

As he punched Play, he saw it in his grandfather's eyes. They were brown, like his dad's, and glistening with desperation as he made his final attempt to reach Jason through words. The pain in his eyes, the quiver in his voice, told the whole story. He would go to his grave with a grief so deep that even death couldn't release him from it.

"I do not blame you for this," his grandfather said into the camera. "The events of that day play in my mind over and over and over again. I'm so sorry. If your father hadn't died while working for me . . . Please give me a chance to explain. Ever since that day, my life has been filled with grief. It is apparent that you will never forgive me. It's also something I cannot do for myself. I loved your father so much . . ."

Red looked down, trying to gather himself, rubbing his knuckles and trying to push through the emotion that was obviously taking him over. "A parent should never have a child precede him in death. It is the most painful experience imaginable . . ."

Suddenly Hamilton stepped behind Red. Jason watched as Red's longtime friend took him by the shoulders and addressed the men behind the camera. "That's enough for today, gentle-men."

The friendship between the men was apparent. His stoic and steely eyed grandfather melted under the hands of his faithful friend. It was a bond Jason couldn't identify with, but wanted. Desperately.

◇ ◇ ◇

Jason took a deep breath as he came around the corner into Emily's room. He wasn't sure what to expect, but he wanted to bring a smile to her face. He stood in the doorway a moment and studied her. She was propped up with pillows, her face turned away from him. She looked thinner and paler. He knocked on the open door.

Emily turned toward him, and a faint smile crossed her lips. "Welcome back, stranger."

"Hey." He smiled and glanced at Alexia, who was knitting in a chair in the corner. She looked pleased to see him.

Jason stepped into the room and reclined across the end of Emily's bed. Her eyes had lost some of their sparkle, and dark circles clung to the skin beneath them. She seemed to be wait-ing for something, so Jason produced from behind his back the doll he'd bought at the airport in South America. "Ta-da."

The doll was colorful enough, but Emily didn't look impressed. "Wow. An airport gift-shop gift." Her expression overemphasized the *du* in *dull.* "How thoughtful. Does it come with needles?"

Jason looked to Alexia for help, but she only chuckled and went back to knitting, shrugging as though she couldn't help him through this one.

Emily studied him intently and said, "Yeah, you can kiss me, even though you're a guy."

Jason leaned in and kissed her as gently as a butterfly landing on a flower. "I missed you too," he whispered.

"Whatever," Emily said, spinning up the attitude. "Let's cut to the chase: you really blew it with us this Christmas."

Jason feigned a serious expression. "I was unavoidably detained."

She seemed to concede that point. "Okay, yeah. But I want Christmas." Then she grabbed Jason's shirt and pulled him close to her. "I want to ride a horse," she whispered.

"Uh, I've got like a week or two left with this other thing, but, um . . . let me make a call and we'll see—"

"Jason," Emily said, her eyes desperate and vulnerable. "Now."

○ ○ ○

Miss Hastings normally wouldn't interrupt, but there was an urgency in Jason's voice she'd never heard before. She knocked on Mr. Hamilton's door and peeked her head in. "Excuse me, sir." Several people surrounding the table with the speakerphone turned to look at her. "It's Jason on line two."

Mr. Hamilton looked at his staff members. "Will you all excuse me? I have to take this call."

The employees quickly gathered their things and stood to leave. Miss Hastings shut the door as Mr. Hamilton punched on the speakerphone.

"Go ahead, Jason."

"Mr. Hamilton, look, one way or another, this is over. Either I was in South America way too long, or I missed the deadline, or whatever. But what I'm about to do is way more important, and I know you have no reason whatsoever to trust me, but I need to borrow my grandfather's jet, and I need it now."

Mr. Hamilton glanced at Miss Hastings, who tried to encourage him to keep listening with a gentle nod.

Jason continued, "I want to take Alexia and Emily to Gus's ranch for a late Christmas."

"Jason," Mr. Hamilton said, "do you know what you're doing? Look, I have no control—"

Miss Hastings couldn't help herself. She leaned toward the speakerphone and for the first time that she could remember actually interrupted her boss. "What, um, Mr. Hamilton was saying was that he'll be sending along Red's next gift on your Conversay. You have your bags packed within the hour, and, uh—" She glanced at Mr. Hamilton's skeptical expression. "—he will have the jet fueled and ready to go."

"Thank you," Jason said. His voice was, for once, full of cheer. "This means so much to me. And Hamilton, I promise I'm going to take back all those nasty thoughts about you being the grinch." Miss Hastings couldn't help the chuckle that escaped. "Thanks again. Merry Christmas!"

○ ○ ○

Jason had always had a strong aversion to Christmas carols, but Emily won him over, and he sang "Jingle Bells" like an out-of-control jovial elf who couldn't carry a tune if his life depended on it. But it kept Emily giggling for a good hour. He was willing to look like a complete idiot just to see that little girl smile.

It was night by the time they arrived at Gus's ranch. Jason thought he'd never want to see this place again, but here he was, and it almost felt like he was coming home.

Alexia gazed out the front windshield of the SUV, her eyes wide with awe. Jason had to admit that he was a little in awe too.

Jason hopped out of the car, and Gus came right out the front door, grinning like Santa Claus.

"Hey, Gus!" Jason called to him, pointing to the lawn. "What is this? Snow in Texas?"

Gus walked down the front steps and across the white lawn. "Had it trucked in. Ho, ho, ho! All right, Hector! Hit it!"

Every inch of his house, including trees, bushes, and the trim on his roof, suddenly glowed with bright, dazzling Christmas lights. "Merry Christmas," Gus said, approaching them.

"Gus, this is Emily."

"Hi, Emily." He shook her hand. "Welcome."

"And Alexia."

"Alexia. How're ya doin'?"

Gus looked back at Jason. "And there he is." He smiled, then pulled him into a hug.

Jason couldn't help but smile back.

"I'll get your bags," Gus said.

Jason watched Emily walk toward the house, her eyes tracing every light. All the colors danced in her eyes. She stooped to scoop up some snow. Alexia moved up next to Jason and leaned into his shoulder. "I see why you chose this place," she said, smiling.

"I wish I could take the credit. Emily said her wish was to go horseback riding."

"What?" Obviously surprised, Alexia shook her head, trying to explain, but her words were choked by sudden emotion.

"What? What's wrong?"

Through a sob, Alexia said, "She's—she's terrified of horses. I'm the one who loves horses."

Jason pulled her close as they regarded the sight before them—a tiny angel playing in the pure white snow.

"Oh, Jason," she said, clutching him, "it's so beautiful. Thank you."

More than anything, he wanted to thank them.

chapter 17

$a$lexia couldn't remember the last time she'd felt this much peace. The country spread far and wide: the grass yellow, the trees one-by-one dropping their leaves, the water still and smooth and sparkling in the morning sun. Cattle wandered from place to place. Alexia put her hand on her horse's neck, feeling the animal's muscles as it carried her along this slice of heaven.

Nearby, Emily rode with Gus right behind her. He gently guided their horse in a slow walk. He'd decorated the horse with antlers in an attempt to put Emily at ease.

"Well," Gus said, gesturing toward land that seemed to roll past the horizon, "this is what I was telling you about. Pretty, huh?"

"It's beautiful," Jason said.

Alexia was afraid her heart wasn't big enough to take it all in. Everywhere she looked there was beauty, from the breathtaking surroundings to her fragile daughter putting on a brave face to make her mom smile. She never wanted to forget this moment. She tried her best to feel all of the emotions swirling inside her, to remember every word her daughter spoke, every smile she gave.

"Hey, come here," Jason said to Alexia as he dismounted his horse. "I want to show you something."

Alexia hesitated. She didn't want to leave Emily. "Gonna be okay, sweetie?"

Emily smiled and leaned into Gus, who gave Alexia a reassuring wink. She dismounted and followed Jason, who walked a few paces and then stopped, fixated on the water hole below. Alexia stood silently next to him. Then he turned to her.

"Alexia, there's something I need to do."

"What?"

His look turned serious. "For Emily."

Then he smiled, and before she could say anything, she found herself immersed in a kiss that absorbed all of her sensibilities— including the fact that her daughter was watching every second of it. But as her lips tingled with delight, she realized that was exactly the purpose of it all. She smiled and drew away from him, but he was apparently not prepared to stop.

"And now for me." He pulled her into another kiss, and Alexia let herself go. What should hold her back? All she had was now.

"And now for Gus," he said teasingly as he came up for air.

And, she thought as she found his lips again, *for me.*

"How 'bout that?" she heard Gus say from his horse.

Yeah. How about that.

○ ○ ○

Jason never thought he'd find himself in a rocker on a porch in the country, but here he was. Out on the lawn, just beyond the edge of the snow, Emily stood beneath the open sky where stars twinkled like they were calling her home. She studied them, her face drawn with curiosity.

Jason pulled out the Conversay and pushed Play.

Red's picture came into view. "When I achieved my dreams, it was like going home to a place I'd never been before. You don't know that feeling, do you? The first few gifts I gave you were practical. Show up, do this, do that. And then the gifts started needing you to provide input. They needed intuition.

"Still, your average person is too weighted down. Jason, you need to be free—free to dream. You need to come up with a dream, then act on it. Jason, this is the time for you to dream."

Putting away the Conversay, Jason stood, walked down the porch steps, and joined Emily as she regarded the sky. "You thinking about butterflies?" he asked.

"No, Jason," she said adamantly. "I'm looking at the stars."

"You know," Jason said, kneeling beside her, "I set this whole thing up because I thought you wanted to go horseback riding, not your mom."

"Get real. Horses are smelly and sweaty."

Jason smiled. "So, sweetie," he asked, "what's your dream? If you could dream of anything, anything, what would *your* dream be?"

Jason halfway expected one of her quips, but instead, her eyes found the stars and she stood still for a moment, giving it serious thought. Then she said, "My dream . . . my dream was a perfect day." She turned and looked down at him. "And I'm just finishing it. My dream was to be with people I love, that love each other, that love me."

Then she fell into his arms and buried her face into his shoulder. Jason scooped her up, wrapping every inch of his arms around her. She cried, and for the first time since he'd known her, she seemed like the tiny, fragile child she really was.

And for the first time in his life, he felt like he could give something.

○ ○ ○

Emily watched the fire crackle and roar in front of her and listened to her mom chat with Gus and his wife. Her body felt sleepy. That's the only way she could describe it. Sometimes her mind would be wide awake but her body wanted to go to sleep. She noticed the Christmas tree twinkling nearby. The smell of apple cider and pumpkin pie floated past her. *This* was how Christmas was supposed to be. Exactly like this.

Jason, wearing a silly Santa hat, plopped down beside her and planted another hat on her head. "You look silly," she said.

"All for you," he replied and put his head on her shoulder.

"What about you, Jason?" she said in a matter-of-fact tone. "What's your dream?"

He thought for a minute. "I don't know. For as long as I could remember, all I wanted to do was have fun. Now I don't have a clue."

"It's okay. Guys are clueless."

Jason laughed. She liked to make him laugh.

"Hey, you have to know this: even if you don't have a dream of your own, you gave me mine. That counts for something."

"Of course," he whispered.

Emily let him stare into the fire a moment longer, then prodded him, gesturing toward the staircase where her mom stood in those silly horse pajamas she'd bought for herself and Emily. Emily wore them just to be nice. She really, really didn't like horses. But she liked her mom, and her mom was smiling, more than she could remember her smiling in a long time. Laughing too. And, she had to admit, horses were growing on her.

She glanced at Jason, who was peeking over the back of the couch with her. "Look at her. Isn't she beautiful? I mean, except for her choice in lipstick." Much too pale for her skin tone. "But you have to admit, even if you got nothing else out of the deal but her, you'd still be a huge winner."

Emily pulled him down to below the back of the couch. "*Don't* blow it. You're likely to do it."

She eyed him, but he looked as though he understood. Completely.

"Merry Christmas, Jason." She gave him a quick peck on the cheek.

He smiled and grazed the back of his pointer finger along her nose. "Merry Christmas."

◇ ◇ ◇

Power suit. Power tie. Gold cuff links. Leather shoes. But for some reason, Jason Stevens didn't feel powerful. In fact, he felt utterly helpless as he stood before the staff of the Hamilton Law Firm.

He'd rehearsed over and over in his head what he wanted to say, but now the words weren't flowing and nothing he said seemed to be coming out right. He stuttered, pronounced a word wrong, and felt perspiration break through his undershirt.

This was nerve racking . . . but it wasn't prison. He smiled. *Come on, Stevens, get a grip. Finish strong.*

"Up until now, I've only existed. I've . . . um . . . I've drifted through life day to day, thinking that was enough. And honestly, I don't know if I have my own dream. But I do know I can help others fulfill theirs. I know it."

Jason studied the faces in the room, all sitting in judgment over him.

Finally, Mr. Hamilton spoke up. "Jason, will you excuse us for a few minutes?"

Miss Hastings escorted Jason out, then closed the door. A secretary sat typing at her desk. Several lush chairs offered him a place to sit, but he couldn't. He could only pace, think, hope . . . pray.

Never had there been a time in his life when he'd bared more of his soul. He had nothing left to give. But had it been enough?

"Jason." Miss Hastings stood in the doorway, beckoning him back in. Jason's fingertips were slick with sweat as he reentered the room. The team looked as though they hadn't moved. They each watched him carefully as he stood again before them.

"We've deliberated and evaluated whether or not your answer conforms with the expressed desires of Red Stevens," Mr. Hamilton said. "And we find that your answer does."

Surprise and relief slipped out by way of a smile.

"Therefore, we are releasing the amount allocated for you at this time. That is, one hundred million dollars, to do with whatever you please."

One hundred *million* dollars? Million? Hamilton slid a check across the table. The simple piece of paper held a powerful set of numbers.

"All of us at the firm want to congratulate you, Jason, for sticking it out, putting up with some very harsh conditions, and prevailing. Congratulations, Jason."

Applause. Applause? For him? Jason didn't know what to say, so he glanced at Miss Hastings, who always seemed to know just what to do. She clasped her hands together and nodded her approval. He didn't have to do anything. He just had to . . . be.

The applause died down, leaving Jason with the strangest feeling. It wasn't that he wasn't overjoyed. It was just that he felt . . . underwhelmed.

"So that's it?" he asked.

"Yes. I think so," Mr. Hamilton said with a small smile.

"No, don't get me wrong," Jason said, looking at all of them. "It's not the amount. It's . . . uh, it's just . . . I don't know. I was expecting a different feeling or something."

Miss Hastings stepped up beside him and patted him on the shoulder. "I think that's because now you are a different person," she said gently.

"And, no," Mr. Hamilton said with a mischievous smile, "we won't cash *that* check for you."

chapter 18

Jason had worked most of the day, barely taking time to eat or even enjoy the fact that his penthouse had been restored. Before, he couldn't wait for it all to be moved back, but now that it was here, it wasn't really worth the time to stop and admire. He had a plan, and he wasn't about to let a one-of-a-kind sofa get in his way.

He'd spent hours talking to architects, bankers, real-estate agents. It was well into the evening and he was now on the phone with a property developer who specialized in parking garages.

"Well," the man was saying, "that would depend on how many vehicles you were talking about."

His other line buzzed. "I'm sorry, can you hold on?"

"Certainly."

"Yeah?" Jason said.

It was his doorman. "Mr. Stevens, a young lady to see you."

"Great. Send her up." Jason clicked back to his other call. "I'm sorry."

"Will there be a large number of—"

"Yeah. There are gonna be plenty of cars."

"Okay, we'll have someone look into it and let you know."

"Okay. Thank you."

Jason hung up the phone. He picked up the check, studying it. Soon he heard footsteps behind him and turned. He was surprised to find Caitlin walking toward him. He hadn't even heard her get off the elevator. And now he couldn't take his eyes off her. Dressed to kill in vintage, Caitlin owned it with a nice dose of cleavage.

He stood to greet her.

She looked around and grinned. "I like the remodel. Where have you been?"

Jason averted his eyes as she moved into his space. "In and out of prison."

"Good to hear." She stepped closer, her face just inches from his. Then she pulled the collar of his shirt down, tracing his chest with her finger. "No visible tattoos. I've missed you." Her eyes sliced sideways, and she noticed the paper on the desk. "What's this?"

"It's nothing," Jason said, snatching it off the desk.

Her eyebrows climbed high on her forehead. "That's a nice

round number. Somehow I don't think you'll be having any more credit-card problems, will you?" Her smile teased him. "You know, you still owe me dinner."

"How could I ever forget?"

"I missed you," she said again. And then she kissed him. Jason didn't pull away. She slid away from him and tossed her hair over her shoulder. "I think I still remember my way around. Why don't you meet me in a few minutes?" And with that, she headed to Jason's bedroom, slinging what was apparently a night bag over her shoulder. Jason knew from experience, she wasn't going to be coming out in pajamas and fuzzy slippers.

As soon as he heard the door click, he hightailed it to the elevator and hit the down button.

Downstairs he called for his driver and jumped into the limo, where he blew out a very loud sigh.

Jim glanced in the rearview mirror. "You okay there, Mr. Stevens?"

"Fine."

"Where to?"

"The park."

"The park?"

"The park."

And it was there that he met his old friend, the park bench. Sitting with his arms folded over its backrest, Jason had the perfect view. And perspective. Here at the park bench it all came full circle, under a starry night. It was time to make his dreams a reality.

○ ○ ○

Mornings invigorated Jason, which was why he'd scheduled the meeting for nine a.m. He gathered his things from the limo. Jim, his driver, asked, "Shall I keep the limo running, Mr. Stevens?" Jason smiled as he marched forward, hearing Jim say, "Maybe not."

In a large conference room he'd reserved, he set the stage for what he knew was going to be quite a show. And soon enough, ten bankers arrived—serious and skeptical, no doubt. They were business associates of his grandfather's, and judging by their expressions, they weren't quite expecting . . . him.

Thankfully he recognized an ally. Two! Mr. Hamilton and Miss Hastings entered, both looking at least mildly impressed.

A surge of confidence made him stand tall. "Ah, Mr. Hamilton. Miss Hastings. I'm so happy you came."

They both glanced around the room. Miss Hastings asked, "Jason . . . what's going on?"

"Have a seat. Please. I insist."

As they did, Jason turned. It was his turn to command the room. "Thank you all for joining me today. May I direct your attention to . . ." Jason lifted the blue sheet covering the canvas that held his . . . dream.

Sketched in subdued colors was what they were sure to perceive as an urban project. And indeed it was. But it was so much more, as evidenced by the lovely woman who had slipped in at the back. Jason met Alexia's eyes, which reassured him that this was what he was born for.

160

Jason turned his attention to the rest of the room. "It's called Emily's Home. It's for a dozen or more families experiencing extraordinary health challenges. Now, over here will be the homes." He revealed another part of the plan. "They're part of the same complex, yet individual dwellings. Families are going to be able to live together while they face their problems. Obviously there's going to be plenty of parking. Over here," he continued, pulling off the third sheet, "is going to be a state-of-the-art employment center catering to parents, single or married, who need to earn some sort of income while their child undergoes treatment."

Jason pointed to the final drawing. "Now at this state-of-the-art hospital . . ." He paused. "Excuse me, what's missing? Oh, yeah. A church." He smiled at Alexia. "A worship center." That had been Emily's idea.

Nobody snickered, at least outwardly. But he could tell by the amused looks on their faces that nobody was taking him seriously. One banker held up a finger. "How much is this going to cost exactly?"

"If you look at the prospectus in front of you, page five, the total initial outlay will be $350 million." That drew a few gasps. "Your part will be to underwrite the financing and a loan guarantee of $250 million." That drew stunned silence. "I'm going to be putting up the first $100 million of my own money."

Jason couldn't help but look at Mr. Hamilton, who nodded his approval.

"Mr. Stevens," one banker said, "this is all well and fine. We did business with your grandfather for many years. But—"

"Excuse me for interrupting, but I didn't phrase this as a question. You *are* going to do this. You made this much off my grandfather in a typical year."

Jason heard the faint ring of a cell phone. The bankers turned to each other. Jason focused on Alexia. Her cell phone rang again just as Mr. Hamilton spoke up.

"And, gentlemen, this project has the full resources of the Hamilton Law Firm backing it. Pro bono, as I'm sure you will be too."

The murmuring began again, but Jason became distracted when he noticed Alexia talking on her cell phone. She was trying to speak in a hushed voice, but her expression did all the talking. Before Jason could do anything, she had rushed from the room.

"Wrap up the details for me, will you, Hamilton?" he asked.

"My pleasure."

"Thank you all. I appreciate it," Jason said. He slipped out of the conference room and stepped out the front doors of the office building just in time to see Alexia speed away in a taxi.

"Hey! Whoa!" But it was too late. She was gone. Jason jumped into his limo and ordered his driver to follow.

Please . . . no . . . not now. Not now.

◇ ◇ ◇

Jason knew his way there well now. He'd visited Emily every single day since their Christmas together. He raced up the stairs because the elevators took a long time during the day, and he took the west, not the east, stairwell because there were fewer turns to get there.

He rounded the corner, but before he reached her room, he heard Alexia's anguished cry. It was the cry of a mother whose child had been ripped from her arms by death. Jason had never heard a cry like it before, and it made his knees weak and his heart shatter instantly. He couldn't comfort her.

All he wanted to do was save her, help her, get Emily back somehow. They'd known they had little time left, but now time had snapped its jaws shut, ending all hope for any more words, any more minutes, any more songs, jokes, laughter . . .

Jason slammed his hand against the wall, squeezing his eyes shut but allowing himself to feel every ounce of the pain. It was the pain Alexia felt, and he wanted to feel it with her. His entire life he'd closed himself off to anything that could hurt him. Now was the time to let himself be wounded by love. There was no greater pain than this, he imagined. None deeper. None so purifying.

Blistering tears ran down his face as all of the memories he had with Emily scourged his heart. He clutched his chest, helpless to do anything but let his soul be cut deeply by this little girl who'd seen past every wall he put up, every flaw he had, and loved him anyway.

With all his might, he tried to stop his tears, tried to compose himself to be strong for Alexia, but he couldn't. All he could offer her was love, and so as nothing but a broken man, he rounded the corner.

Through her tears, Alexia looked into his face and said, "She wanted me to be there. It was so important to her. She wanted me to be there . . ."

Jason wasn't sure how much time passed, but finally Alexia took his hand and led him out of the room.

They walked, clutching each other, down to the chapel Emily loved so much.

He held Alexia, but deep in his heart he knew somewhere, somehow, Emily held them both.

chapter 19

J ason and Alexia, as mayor of Charlotte, it is my extreme honor and privilege to preside over the groundbreaking for Emily's Home. But it is also a sad day, in that the namesake and the inspiration for this incredible project is not here with us today. But her spirit will always be with us all . . ."

The words echoed in Jason's mind as he walked toward the conference room with Mr. Hamilton, Miss Hastings, and several assistants. At the groundbreaking, Mr. Hamilton, in earshot of everyone, had said, "I'm so proud of the man you've become." Jason wasn't sure if he'd ever been paid a higher compliment with more meaning. And he'd become this man thanks, in great part, to Hamilton, a man he'd once considered an enemy.

"I understand you went outside the boundaries of our instructions with one of those gifts," Mr. Hamilton said abruptly.

"What?" Jason asked, caught off guard.

"Don't *what* me," Hamilton said, eyeing him. "You know what I'm talking about."

Just then they reached the conference room, and Jason noticed a man placing a mini-DVD on the long table. Jason recognized the man as the private investigator who had been following him to make sure he obeyed all of Red's rules.

"Miss Hastings, will you dismiss everyone, please?" Mr. Hamilton asked.

"Yes, sir."

When the three of them were alone in the room, Mr. Hamilton handed Miss Hastings the DVD. She put it into the player, and as the room grew dark, Jason saw on the screen the grainy, handheld-video images of himself trying every way possible to get money, collecting dimes and quarters any way he could. He'd been trying to raise an extra hundred dollars to cover Alexia's rent. But that probably wasn't going to be a good excuse.

The private investigator's voice came on. "Over the course of several days, this investigator personally witnessed and recorded the subject as he committed various misdemeanor infractions, for which he was never cited. Nevertheless, illegal activities did occur: panhandling, bordering on assault; stealing private property; resale of stolen items; street vending without a permit . . ."

On and on he went as Jason watched himself dig for coins in and under slot returns, then sell flowers. That had been a low point. He'd been pathetic about it, too, asking people to buy two or even three, whatever he could get out of them, making up all kinds of stories to gain sympathy.

". . . It is the opinion of this investigator that the subject is a reprobate and incapable of completing the twelve gifts laid out in Red Stevens' will."

"That's enough, Miss Hastings," Mr. Hamilton said.

"My pleasure, Mr. Hamilton," she replied.

The lights came up, and Jason was surprised to find Mr. Hamilton smiling. Miss Hastings too.

"Jason," Mr. Hamilton said, "if you made it this far, he had one final message."

He gestured to a door that was slightly open. Jason stood and walked toward it. It felt a little surreal as he slowly stepped in. The room was smaller than he'd imagined. The camera still sat on its tripod, aimed at the empty chair.

Except it wasn't empty. His grandfather sat there, and Jason imagined what he might have to say.

"Jason?"

"Yeah?"

"You gave away the hundred million?"

"Yeah. So what?"

"Well, if you are standing here now it means that not only have you succeeded in receiving all of my gifts, but have done so beyond the boundaries that I have set. I guess that means that I have succeeded as well. What I could not accomplish in life, I

167

have done in death. As long as you are still alive, I will be, too."

Jason swallowed back tears. He wanted to reach out and hug him, hold him, be held by the man who used to pick him up and swing him around in the air as a young boy. Now all he had to hold on to was . . . honor. And Jason knew it was enough.

"I love you . . . son."

"I love you, too."

"Goodbye, Jason."

Climbing into the chair, Jason sat where his grandfather had taught him the greatest lesson of his life. And he wept.

◇ ◇ ◇

"Jason?"

Jason looked up from where he sat in Red's chair. "Yes?"

"You okay?"

Jason nodded a little. "Just thinking about him. Trying to imagine him in this little room." He smiled at Hamilton.

"Why don't you come out here for a moment?"

Hamilton, followed by Jason, returned to his chair. Jason noticed the wooden box that had started his whole journey sitting on the table. Hamilton opened it and pulled out a piece of paper, then held it up so he could read it clearly. "As executor of the estate of Red Stevens, I hereby execute and otherwise assign complete and controlling interest to Jason Stevens the balance of Red's estate, including all holdings, investment portfolios, and offshore interests, totaling in excess of two billion dollars."

With all Jason had been through, he wasn't sure there was too much more in life that could leave him stunned, but he was wrong, to the point that he was speechless.

"Depending on OPEC prices and foreign currency fluctuations, of course," Hamilton added in true form.

Jason laughed. Of course.

◦ ◦ ◦

Hamilton sat in a leather chair in his office, studying an old picture of himself with Red. They'd been two handsome fellows back in the day.

He stood and walked to the window, and his mind wandered back to that fateful phone call. "I need a lawyer for a few business ideas I have, a few still in the dream stage."

"When would you like to meet?"

"Meet? Hell, you're hired!"

"Sir, are you sure you wouldn't like to meet first?"

"You were at the top of your law class, were you not?"

"Yes, sir."

"Then you're my lawyer. Now, let's get on with it. We got a world to conquer."

Behind him, Hamilton heard Miss Hastings enter his office. She came up beside him. Glancing at her, he asked, "Do you think I'm old, Miss Hastings?"

With her usual elegance, she shook her head.

"Well, I think it's about time I retire from this law firm."

With a knowing smile, she asked, "What ever will you do, Mr. Hamilton?"

"Go to work with Jason Stevens. Change the world."

◇ ◇ ◇

Jason sat on his old friend, the park bench. Red had Hamilton. Jason had Park Bench. It had become a place where he could think and listen. He so badly wanted to hear Emily's voice, her attitude, her impolite observations about him and his world. But instead, most often, he heard her heart, and it told him to keep going, to take care of her mom, and to keep living his dream.

Jason looked up to find Alexia walking toward him. He would never get tired of seeing that beautiful smile. "Hi," he said.

She slid onto the bench beside him. "Hi."

He looked into her eyes.

"Thank you," he told her.

He pictured Emily with her hand on her hip and that little umbrella propped up on her shoulder, twirling it impatiently and saying, "Kiss her, you idiot."

So he kissed her, and a butterfly dipped through the air, fluttering across the Charlotte skyline and toward the heavens.

Coming Soon!
New UniWyo Debit Cards

New UniWyo Debit Card

VISA

UNI WYO
FEDERAL CREDIT UNION

Valid thru
00/00

1234 1234 1234 1234

UniWyo Member

Important Dates:

- ## Week of May 21st:

  Look for your NEW DEBIT CARD in the mail with your NEW PIN number to follow 2 days afterward.

- *June 3rd: Last day to use old card*

- *June 4th: First day to use new card*

Please note: Your old PIN number will NOT be usable with your new card.

For more information, please call UniWyo at 307-721-5600 or visit www.uniwyo.com

UniWyo Federal Credit Union
1610 E. Reynolds St.
Laramie, WY 82072

002 / 02197

SHEILA P S CLARK,
2125 CURTIS STREET
LARAMIE WY 82070-

Reading Group Guide

1. All of the survivors in Red Stevens's family seem to be pretty despicable—greedy, materialistic, and petulant. Do you know any families like this? What do you think makes people act this way?

2. As you observe Red's children and grandchildren as the story begins, what opinion do you form about the kind of person Red must have been? What mistakes did he make as a parent? Why do Red's family and Mr. Hamilton view him so differently?

3. Jason's first gift was the gift of work. Do you think of your work as a gift? If not, how do you view it?

4. The second gift was the gift of friends. How would you define a true friend? What importance do you put on friendship in your life?

5. When Jason received his paycheck—the gift of money—he was incensed that the check was so small. Then he was asked to "spend it on someone experiencing a real problem." If you were asked to do the same with your next paycheck, what do you think you would do with it? Up until then, what had money bought him and his family?

6. Jason went to Thanksgiving dinner with the faint hope of being able to turn the day into something more civil than usual. His hopes were quickly dashed. Have you ever gone into a family gathering with the goal of bringing harmony out of what is usually discord? How did you handle the situation? What was the outcome?

7. Red said, "Learning is a gift. Even if pain is your teacher." How did this play itself out in Jason's experience in Ecuador? What did he learn about his dad? His grandfather? Himself?

8. What was Red Stevens's ultimate gift to Jason?

9. If you had to choose between receiving a gift of ten billion dollars and the non-monetary gifts Jason received, which would you choose?

10. Read the list of twelve gifts on page 181. How many of those gifts have you received in your life? How has the value of those gifts changed in your mind since reading *The Ultimate Gift*?

Note from Rene Gutteridge

I had just dropped off my daughter at preschool when I got a call asking if I would be interested in writing a novelization of a movie. After some discussion, I decided that this would be a good project for me. I had studied screenwriting in college, but had moved into writing novels shortly afterward. I thought it would be interesting to adapt a screenplay into a novel.

I was sent a copy of *The Ultimate Gift* overnight to watch. For once we didn't have anything going on that evening, so we put the kids to bed, popped some popcorn, and stuck the movie in, eager to see what, exactly, this movie was all about. I'm not sure what I was expecting, but I can tell you what I wasn't expecting . . . to be crying like a baby at the end! The movie was incredibly moving and my husband and I sat afterward in awe, barely able to put into words what we'd experienced. The acting, writing, and directing were beyond superb.

But more than that, the movie touched us personally. My family and I were facing challenges that tested our strength, perseverance, and faith.

The message of *The Ultimate Gift* deeply inspired me, even beyond the theme of giving and love and self-sacrifice. Through it, God comforted me, assuring me that all of our problems, in His gentle hands, are a gift that, as A.W. Tozer puts it, have the "power to purify, to detach, to humble, to destroy the fear of death and, what is more important to you at the moment, the fear of life . . . sometimes pain can do what even joy cannot, such as exposing the vanity of earth's trifles . . ." All we had been through, all we would face in the future, would be used for our good, to teach us what it means to really live. As the character of Red Stevens puts it, "You haven't really lived until you've lost everything."

So *The Ultimate Gift* went from a project to a passion. I have been blessed beyond words to be a part of this extraordinary experience and to work with an extraordinary man such as Jim Stovall. He has been a gift to many. *The Ultimate Gift* turned out to be a gift to me. May it be the start to a wonderful journey of giving for you!

Vision statement about
The Ultimate Gift
from movie producer, Rick Eldridge

The *Ultimate Gift* book was given to me by two of my teenage sons . . . from a financial planner who was mentoring my sons at the time. A month later on a flight from the east coast to the west coast, I opened the book for the first time. By the time we landed in LA, I had finished the book and begun imagining the screenplay. We secured rights to the book and began the quest of all independent filmmakers of crafting the right script, securing funding, and then putting together the right cast and crew to tell the story. It is always a long and tedious process.

Because of the legacy message of this story and the unusual success of the book selling without a major publisher, there was significant interest in a potential film project. With the assistance of several partners—Elim Group, Helixx Group, Legacy Boston, and author Jim Stovall—we were able to secure funding for initial development. And finally, through the visionary leadership of Jim Davis and Stanford Financial Group, we completed the funding to make this film a reality.

The beauty of Jim Stovall's book was the ability to make the characters and elements of the story come alive, allowing the readers to place themselves into the journey as the twelve gifts unfold through the story. The challenge we had was taking this very episodic twelve gift formula and creating a dramatic and compelling feature film structure. Through the crafting of the story by writer Cheryl McKay and director Michael Sajbel, we were able to accomplish this difficult task.

Our vision as a production team was to create a story that would challenge and motivate the viewers to make a difference: to understand the concept of their importance and responsibility to humanity . . . and their unique abilities to affect change by using their gifts in positive ways to influence and better the lives of those around them. This truly is "The Ultimate Gift."

Share the gift . . . change the world.

Vision statement about
The Ultimate Gift
from movie director, Michael O. Sajbel

Since making a film takes a year minimum, often twice that, out of a director's life, I choose the projects I undertake with careful consideration. Ask my wife. I turned down a six-figure salary once in the middle of remodeling.

I was first attracted to the title itself: *The Ultimate Gift.* I think that deep down we all have a feeling that if we only had more of a certain commodity we'd be much better off, that our problems would disappear. Usually it's money, and of course, all it can buy. But life tells us something completely different. Wisdom is knowledge that often is in conflict with what the world believes. A favorite source of inspiration for me says, "A generous person will prosper; he who refreshes others will himself be refreshed."

Of course so many good stories from the beginning of time tell us so. It is more important to give than to receive. The true meaning of anything has to do with character and values and sharing and giving. And this is what attracted me to the book and the characters and the project more than anything else. I also learned early on in my education that you cannot sell something unless you believe in it yourself. So the crucial first step for me was that I believed in the message of *The Ultimate Gift.*

The process of getting hired to direct a film may be a mystery to most, but I'll briefly tell you what I went through. I didn't read any of the screenplays that had been written before I went straight to the source, Jim Stovall's brief yet heartfelt novel. I read it several times and marked it up with highlight pens, notes, and comments. For me to take on a project there has to be a compelling story, a "spine," I term it, and there has to be redemption of some sort. I want each character to go through changes, through tremendous loss, and come out changed and better. Jim's novel had all of this. It resonated with me. It also had an element of fun as well as truth.

I loved the premise: a hard-as-nails yet remorseful billionaire who comes to the end of his time and realizes he needs to do something in death that he could not accomplish in life. A gamble for him, to be sure, as there is no way for him to stick around to make any adjustments should his final plan fail. But I also thought it important to raise the stakes for Jason, the recipient of the gift, to end up in a test for his life where money could not possibly help him and where his adversary didn't even understand his pleading. Through all of this loss comes redemption and gain for all the characters.

I also imagined what each character was like. Were the people in the book the same as the characters in my head? I owed the producers an honest assessment of my vision should a character not line up with someone in the book. For example, I wanted the little girl, Emily, to be almost gothic, wearing Edwardian clothing with a color palate on the dark side. I did not want her to be just another "sweet little girl dying of Leukemia." I wanted grandson Jason (the original book had him as a nephew, I believe, as did early scripts) not what everyone seemed to imagine, in the standard sixties' mode of the rebellious guy who hates his family for their wealth, etc. I said, "This guy embraces his wealth. He cannot function without it, on the surface or at the very core of his being." Fortunately for all of us, I only departed in a few, necessary areas where it was important in translating Jim's written word to the visual language of the screen.

Finally, when you audition to direct, you walk in the door with ideas on casting. This helps explain vision and translation from the written page just as much as anything else. A confession that all of the producers already know: I walked into the door saying that I wanted James Garner to play Red. I wanted the no-nonsense character of Mr. Hamilton to be African American and wanted a seasoned actor for that role. These early casting ideas clarified to the producers what I had in mind, or to put it another way, what my vision was for the project.

After I was hired, many other casting ideas came as a result of the very talented casting people as well as the producers agreeing and really going after the people we *all* wanted. Jason had to be played, in my mind, by someone who had experienced tremendous wealth in his own life. I couldn't afford for anyone to fake that. Drew Fuller was perfect for the role. What a joy it was to find Abigail Breslin to be available for Emily. She shaped the film as much as anyone else. Brian Dennehy was just getting off a play in London and was convinced to do the project based on our final, strong screenplay. I could go on.

Most of all, my vision for this project was to take Jim's novel and make his initial vision "visual" and to keep the story fresh and exciting. I'm glad that Rick Eldridge and all of the other producers agreed. I am very proud of this film. To anyone and everyone who worked on the film and helped make it what it is today, you were a gift to me. (Admit it, you were expecting me to say something like this.)

The 12 Gifts

The Gift of Work
He who loves his work never labors.

The Gift of Money
Money is nothing more than a tool. It can be a force of good, a force of evil, or simply be idle.

The Gift of Friends
It is a wealthy person, indeed, who calculates riches not by gold but by friends.

The Gift of Learning
Education is a lifelong journey whose destination expands as you travel.

The Gift of Problems
Problems can only be avoided by exercising good judgment . . . Good judgment can only be attained by experiencing life's problems.

The Gift of Family
Some people are born into wonderful families. Others have to find or create them. Being a member of a family is a priceless privilege that costs nothing but love.

The Gift of Laughter
Laughter is good medicine for the soul. Our world is desperately in need of more such medicine.

The Gift of Dreams
Faith is all that dreamers need to see the future.

The Gift of Giving
The only way you can truly get more out of life for yourself is to give part of yourself away.

The Gift of Gratitude
In those times when we yearn to have more in our lives, we should dwell on the things we already have. In doing so, we will often times find that our lives are already full to overflowing.

The Gift of a Day
Life at its essence boils down to one day at a time. Today is the day!

The Gift of Love
Love is a treasure for which we can never pay. The only way we keep it is to give it away.

Interview with James Garner
(played Red in the movie)

Interviewer:

Red is the heart and foundation of the movie in the sense that he sets the story emotionally.

James Garner:

You've got a dead man setting something in motion . . .

Interviewer:

Tell me about it. What is his plan for Jason?

James Garner:

Well, I can't tell you what his plan is because then you'll know the whole script, but he sends him off to learn about work and people and life in general. And he makes him run a merry chase to learn about what really matters before he gives him the ultimate gift.

Interviewer:

Is he a self-made man?

James Garner:
Red made his fortune in the cattle business early in his life and branched out to about everything else. He probably owned insurance companies, and all that, because he was an extremely wealthy man.

Interviewer:
What is Red's biggest failure?

James Garner:
Family was his biggest failure. And he's a little disappointed about them, except Jason, his grandson whom he really cared for.

Interview:
What do you think it was about Jason?

James Garner:
Well, we're getting way into the character here and into the movie, but Jason's father, who would be my son, was killed and my character felt guilty about that. To tell any more would give too much away, but as Red would say, "You don't really begin to live until you've lost it all."

Interview with Brian Dennehy
(played Gus in the movie)

Interviewer:

Tell me how the character Gus fits into the overall story of *The Ultimate Gift*.

Brian Dennehy:

The whole point about Gus is that he's a good man. He's a hard-working decent man who believes in hard work, has achieved a lot in his life through hard work and his relationship with his old friend Red.

Red knows that he will help his grandson find his way out of this mess that he's gotten himself into. It's not just a legal mess, it's more importantly a crisis of the soul and spirit.

Interviewer:

When Jason first arrives and asks Gus for his "gift," how does he react?

Brian Dennehy:

Oh, he just laughs at him. He just thinks it's funny. Because, of course, the gift that they're talking about can't be given, its got to be earned. And the kid doesn't really have any idea what that process is, nor does the audience at that point. They realize it, hopefully, approximately at the same time that Jason does. Which is that the gift is a process—not a thing.

Interviewer:
Gus really starts the process and ends the process.

Brian Dennehy:
Well, Gus realizes the process is over only when the lesson has been learned. And, of course, that's also when it's time for this kid to move on. Gus's life—while valuable, moral, and strong—is not, Jason's life. He has to live his own life . . . find a way of living that life, and hopefully, he has. It is time for school to be out and for him to start living his own life.

Interviewer:
From what I've seen watching you rehearse today, you seem very comfortable with the role of Gus. It seems very easy for you. Have you found anything that was a challenge in the role?

Brian Dennehy:
Well, I still have to do the rope gag this afternoon, and that'll probably be a problem. I've used a lariat in the past, but it's been a long time and I'm not really a roper. And it's windy today. So, yeah, that'll be a challenge!

Interview with Drew Fuller
(played Jason in the movie)

Interviewer:

How did you hear about plans to film the movie *The Ultimate Gift*?

Drew Fuller:

I'd just been shooting a movie in Europe for three months, and I'd been home for about two. I got ahold of the script and I woke up one morning, rolled over in my bed, sat up, read the script, cried my eyes out, and then called my manager and said, "I have to meet them immediately. I love this project. It's amazing. It's like the dream role. I want to do this, I want to go ride the motorcycles, I want to be in prison, and I want to have the penthouse, and I want to drive this sick muscle car. It's just awesome. And I want to cry, and I want to feel, and I want to lose myself and find myself and the whole thing." And they said, "Good. Go do well in the meeting."

Interviewer:

I hear you have a unique approach for feeling at home whenever you travel for a movie?

Drew Fuller:

Yeah. Whenever I leave town to go do a movie—I was born and raised in Los Angeles—I have a tendency to cut myself off from my friends, my family, my life because I'm going to a new place where I become a new character. That new place is my new home. The people there are my family, my friends. If I keep thinking about home and what I'm missing, then it's not fair to the character or to the story. We [actors] have the greatest gift in the world. I mean, I get paid to play for a living. And I love that. I try to live it up as much as I can and be as present as possible.

Interviewer:

How do you view your responsibility as an actor?

Drew Fuller:

It's a huge responsibility. This character has five, six, seven layers. Just when you think you've hit a new level, you dig a little deeper and there's another level there. And to be involved in a script that's opening me up to that . . . that's what it's all about. Pushing me. I'm uncomfortable. I'm nervous. I get scared before I go on set, because I'm hitting levels and I'm doing things I've never done before, things that I've never had to do. And the fact that I've been challenged in this way, and hopefully living up to the challenge, and meeting each one as they come, is very gratifying. So when this is all said and done and the final product is out there, I know that I approached it with my heart and soul and gave it my best. And it has definitely pushed me to a new level as an actor. It has changed me forever. I mean, granted, the story is the one that changes people because it's such a beautiful tale.

Interviewer:
How close has your own life been to the character Jason?

Drew Fuller:
I am no where near a billionaire's grandson, but I was fortunate to be raised in Newport Beach, California, the orange curtain, or the bubble, as some people like to refer to it in Southern California, because it's like this little bubble, country club right on the beach. I mean, my first period in high school was surfing. It's ridiculous and amazing. And the cars in my high school were Mercedes and BMWs, the latest and greatest lifted trucks, and awesome muscle cars. Anything and everything. I saw what money could do to so many people.

I think I've lost contact with almost every single person from my high school except for two. But I saw how it affected these kids. Now when I go home to visit my parents, who still live there, I can see it. It's worse now, but maybe that's because I'm older and more mature. I can see how spoiled everyone is. A lot of it is really ugly.

That's what Jason is trying to hide, that ugliness. He has this really sleek façade of the coolest, most amazing tools, the most beautiful . . . the coolest apartment. So that was my bridge. That was Drew bridging to Jason. And after that, I treat each character like an island, you know. Where I'm at and where the character in the story needs to be. So I find my bridge to get there, and once I'm there, the bridge goes away and I build my character from the ground up.

Interviewer:
How was it to work with James Garner?

Drew Fuller:
What can you say? He's a legend. He's done well over a hundred movies. We actually only filmed one scene together for just one day. It was a surreal moment— in the same vein as *Field of Dreams.* In the scene, it was like his material body was in front of me, but really it was just an image on a screen. I don't think it's sunk in yet. We're acting opposite each other and I'm crying and he's crying and we just give each other this huge hug at the end. After our scene, he took me to dinner at Cracker Barrel. I got sick mid-meal because he was force feeding me all this food like country-fried steak, gravy, fried okra, dumplings . . . it was a disaster! And he was just laughing.

Another legend is Brian Dennahy. On the set, Dennahy came to the conclusion that this is his 117th film. He's great. Oh man, in one of his first scenes he comes out of the house with the Brian Dennahy smile and the "ho ho ho" . . . I was thinking "Yes, that's the Dennahy I know. That's the guy I saw in the movies." Amazing actor. Huge theater actor. He just came off of eight months in London doing "Death of a Salesman" where he just got nominated for an Olivier, which is the equivalent to a Tony in America. He's this amazing theater actor. I relished every moment. I wouldn't leave the set; I just watched what he did.

You couldn't have gotten a better cast. Everyone is so perfect for their role.

Interviewer:

Do you think that one of the 12 gifts stands out as "the ultimate gift"?

Drew Fuller:

No, they're all equally important. Every single "gift" that Jason receives is a necessity. He needs each to progress, to become a man, to have a real sense of soul. He needs to embody and over-come all these things. So there's not one that sticks out more than another or resonates most with me. I've treated them all as equally important because they were all issues that needed to be dealt with.

Interviewer: Is there an essential message to this movie?

Drew Fuller:

Yes, there is but I think I'd like to keep that to myself. Each person will leave the theater taking something from the story. And maybe one particular gift will resonate with them. As a character approaching it, all the gifts are equally important. But as a viewer, it might be one gift, "the gift of work" for instance, resonates with you. Maybe it is something you need to address in your life. I hope everyone takes something from it and be motivated to change something about themselves for the greater good.

Interviewer:
You say you make a place your home. What's it like shooting in Charlotte?

Drew Fuller:
I wish I knew. I've had maybe six days off since I've been here, so I really haven't had a chance to explore. What I've seen of it, I love. Everyone's really friendly. I love that there's an actual season called fall. Leaves are turning colors and all of a sudden trees aren't green anymore. They're red and brown. You just don't have that in LA. I talked to my parents yesterday, and it's 87 degrees there. That's beautiful and nice and fantastic, but . . . it's November, it's Thanksgiving, I want cold, I want scarves, I want red trees, I want crunchy leaves on the ground. I guess it's old fashioned, but Charlotte has all that. I like how crisp the air is and how sweet everyone is. But I don't think I could ever live in any place like this full time. I respond too much to energy, to action. I want to be in the thick of things.

Interview with Abigail Breslin
(played Emily in the movie)

Interviewer:

You play the character Emily. Who is she and what is she like?

Abigail Breslin:

Emily is a very strong and determined girl. She speaks her mind and has just a little bit of an attitude. She has stuff to say, and she wants to say it.

Interviewer:

Can you give me an example of a time when she has an attitude?

Abigail Breslin:

Yes. Most of the time she says things like "What, you can't do that!" or something similar. Emily just says whatever she wants, she doesn't care. She doesn't really mind if somebody doesn't like what she says, she says it anyway.

Interviewer:

Are you anything like Emily?

193

Abigail Breslin:

I'm like Emily because I will say what I feel, but not exactly how she says them. I'll say things that are on my mind.

Interviewer:

What about your hair? You wore a wig in the film, right?

Abigail Breslin:

Yeah. Emily has leukemia, so I had to wear a wig in the movie. But this is my real hair. So we always have to braid it, and then we put this cap on over it, tie knots in it, put on a wig, and pin that, and most of the time put on a hat. So it takes a while. But she has leukemia, and she's dying, so that's basically why she says all the things she wants to say, because she wants to get it out before her time is up.

Interviewer:

Talk a little bit about Emily's attitude on being sick.

Abigail Breslin:

Emily tries not to think about dying, she tries to think about better things. Like living. She isn't focused on when she's going to die, she thinks about how long she has to live. That's what her real attitude about it is. She tries to act in the most positive way.

Interviewer:

Tell me about the first time Emily sees Jason.

Abigail Breslin:

Emily is at a funeral the first time that she sees Jason. She's sort of just standing there, looking around her. She sees Jason coming, who looks kinda cool, he has these sunglasses on, and everybody's real quiet, they're all dressed in black, and they're all sad. He just comes in and acts all cool, and Emily thinks he's cool.

Interviewer:

Why do you think Emily likes Jason? Why is she willing to be his friend?

Abigail Breslin:

Because he's very full of life. And he's always thinking about how he's going to live and what's going to happen to him.

Interviewer:

Why does Emily want her mom to date Jason?

Abigail Breslin:

Emily tries to matchmake with Jason and Alexia so her mom won't be lonely when Emily dies. She wants her to have somebody there with her. And I've done some matchmaking before, so it's kind of fun for me.

Interviewer:

What was one of your favorite scenes to shoot?

195

Abigail Breslin:

One of my favorite scenes was when I had to say to Jason, "It's not complicated, it's pathetic. How can one possibly conceive that I would want to go to Disneyworld?" And that was really fun because I would never say that to anybody. I would get in trouble for saying that to somebody. It was fun being a little bit different from how you are. A little bit 'baddy,' that was kinda fun.

Interviewer:

What if you said it to your real mom?

Abigail Breslin:

If I said it to my. . . I wouldn't say it to my real mom. If I did . . . I wouldn't even think about saying that. I don't know what would happen. I wouldn't say that at all to anybody. And I do, actually, like to go to Disneyland. I just wouldn't say that in real life.

Interviewer:

Tell us how it's been working with Drew Fuller.

Abigail Breslin:

Oh. He throws so many temper tantrums. He like kicks his feet in the air and says everything . . . no, just kidding about that. He's really nice. It's like working with a big brother.

Interviewer:

Is it true he asked you to marry him?

interview with Abigail Breslin

Abigail Breslin:

Yes, he did ask me to marry him. I said no.

Interviewer:

How's it been having Ali as your on-screen mom?

Abigail Breslin:

Ali is really, really nice. And she's funny, and so it's been a lot of fun working with her. We went to a pumpkin patch, actually, to pick up pumpkins for Halloween and that was a lot of fun.

Interviewer:

Heard you had a dance.

Abigail Breslin:

Yeah, we like to dance. (*Does head movements*) We both like music a lot.

Interviewer:

What similarities are there between Emily and Abby?

Abigail Breslin:

We both have a different sense of style. We both have our own style. Emily's more like Gothic, and I'm more Bohemian. One time somebody called me like a little bit of a tomboy, but a girl girl so they called me tomgirl.

Interviewer:

If one of your friends came up to you and asked what *The Ultimate Gift* is about, what would you say?

Abigail Breslin:

The Ultimate Gift is about what's most important to you in your life.

Interviewer:

How does Emily handle being sick?

Abigail Breslin:

Emily has concerns about dying, but she doesn't really care about it as much as she cares about the people that she's leaving behind. And she wants them to be taken care of.

Interviewer:

At the end of the movie when Emily dies, what does Jason do?

Abigail Breslin:

When Emily dies, Jason takes all the money that was so important to him, and he uses it to build a house for sick children. It is called Emily's House. He makes it so that children can stay there when they're sick and get all the help they need. Even though Emily dies, it's sort of like she's still there. She's actually helping other children that are sick and need help.

Interview with Ali Hillis
(played Alexia in the movie)

Interviewer:

What does the ultimate gift mean to you?

Ali Hillis:

I think the ultimate gift is about learning life lessons. I think it is about searching yourself to find some semblance of truth and sincerity in the world. I think *The Ultimate Gift* is going to mean something different to everyone that sees it.

Interviewer:

Your character, Alexia, who is she?

Ali Hillis:

Alexia is the mother of a little girl who is dying of leukemia. She spends a lot of time dealing with her daughter's illness. Then Jason walks into her life, and he's searching for something. Initially I become a tool in his journey, and then after a while I become more than a tool.

Interviewer:
Tell me a little about the relationship between Emily, your character's daughter, and Jason. They appear to have a nice dynamic.

Ali Hillis:
In doing my research, when a parent has a child who is dying, they may be more willing to let the child experience things. So when Emily and Jason first meet, she thinks he is a little scary since he's apparently a homeless person. But Alexia takes a step back and once she feels like she's created a safe distance between them, she watches them relate to each other. Alexia starts to trust this little relationship that is developing. And then, of course, the spitfire Emily has a little deal that she wants to make with Jason, and Jason has a little deal he wants to make with her.

Emily doesn't have a lot of time to make a whole lot of friends since she is in the hospital so much, so it's neat to watch her learn to trust people. And I think as she learns to trust Jason, Alexia is also learning to trust Jason. It becomes more than trust when she starts to see a little bit more into his soul. I think she has very good instincts about him and knows that he is probably a good guy at heart. But she has to find that out slowly.

Interviewer:
Your character is pretty heavy. What do you like about Alexia?

Ali Hillis:
When I first got the script, I was under a pile of scripts at the time,

and unfortunately I had to skim through each script fairly quickly. But I started slowing down as I was turning the pages of *The Ultimate Gift.* I immediately fell in love with Alexia's character because of the relationship she had with her daughter. Here was a woman who obviously had a child very young, and that forced her to be very responsible at a young age. I think she was living vicariously through her daughter in that she was allowing Emily to be a little bit freer so she could really experience life. Alexia was also coming to terms with the fact that her daughter was not going to be around very much longer.

Interviewer:
How did you prepare for your character?

Ali Hillis:
There are a lot of heavy scenes in this movie for Alexia, and, in my opinion, she has it the toughest because she's losing her child. I've never watched a child pass or suffer through a really extraordinary disease so relating to the character and figuring out how to find that place inside of me was definitely a challenge. It's a very specific place inside myself that I have to go to find the essence of what it would feel like to lose a child, and I hope I found that.

Interviewer:
How was it working with the director, Michael Sajbel?

Ali Hillis:

I want to say one thing about the writer first, and then I'll talk about Michael. Jim Stovall wrote a beautiful book that so thoroughly fleshes out these characters that finding the essence of Alexia was not very difficult. It's all on the page, it's all in the words, and it's all in the character building in the story. He just built a beautifully simple story. I love it.

Michael Sajbel, the director, and I go way back. We're both Packer fans, so we have a lot in common. He's a really fun director to work with because he always has a smile on his face. Well, almost always. And he's got a great smile. He sets up the scenes so well. He's great at making sure the actors are prepared. In filming, we shoot out of order for the most part, so he reminds us what happened just before this scene and what is going to happen after this scene, and he gives us little specific essences of little beats he would like us to hit. And then he just lets us play the music. That's nice.

Interviewer:
How was it working with Drew Fuller?

Ali Hillis:
I really enjoy working with Drew. The very first time I met Drew Fuller was in a callback for this movie, and I think we had chemistry right off the bat. It was an interesting chemistry because I think he truly has pieces of himself that he's able to use in this character. And then he's able to soften those pieces and create the person that I had to fall in love with. It's won-

derful to watch him on-site because he really embodies each piece of this character as it goes through the cycle of receiving the ultimate gift.

Interviewer:
Tell us a little about working with Abigail.

Ali Hillis:
I'd never played a mom before. I have a dog, but I don't know if that counts. Abby is fantastic. From the minute I met her, we hit it off. We went to the pumpkin patch on our day off. We took a hay bale ride, we got to pick out four pumpkins, and somehow we ended up with twelve. Don't know how that happened. We got to see baby goats, sheep, and lambs. I think that was the most fun we had and that was off camera! Abby's a very open spirit. She likes to talk about television shows, and I don't know, things that kids talk about. She's just a normal, but absolutely not normal, very special little girl. She makes it pretty easy to play her mom.

Interviewer:
Tell me about working in Charlotte.

Ali Hillis:
I couldn't be happier. I'm so lucky. I had just gotten back from shooting a film in Malta. Where's Malta? I don't even know where it is. But I was there. And I came back pretty exhausted and had a lot of scripts dumped in my lap. As soon as I looked at the front

of *The Ultimate Gift* and noticed it was being shot in Charlotte, North Carolina, and took place in Charlotte, North Carolina, I was there. I hadn't even opened the book, and I said I'll do it. I'm from Charlotte, so shooting here is fantastic. It's a beautiful city and everyone here is so kind and generous and excited about shooting films. Everyone I've met on this production has been nothing but nice. It's been a nice little break from the normalcy of this industry, where people don't have time to get to know each other. But coming to Charlotte has been a nice break for me. I'm staying at home with my parents; I have my dog here with me. It's perfect.

Interview with Lee Meriwether
(played Miss Hastings in the movie)

Interviewer:

What do you think is the central message to this story?

Lee Meriwether:

One is that you should never give up on someone. Goodness is in everyone, you just have to find a way to bring it out. And, Red Stevens, James Garner, found a way after death to bring out the best in Jason.

The movie has adventure, a charming love story, and caring individuals who love one another and yet have a difficult time getting through to one another. People will relate to that.

Interviewer:

It's hard to determine if we, as parents, are setting good examples for our children regarding materialism. Tell me some of your thoughts about this.

Lee Meriwether:

Well, I think all of us have at times wondered whether we're doing the right things for our children. Are we giving them, per-haps, too much monetarily, as opposed to maybe love and affec-tion? This film is so reaffirming because it says as long as there's love, it's all right to give your children certain things. And if they aren't responsible enough to handle it, then you must take it away from them.

Interviewer:
You said that one of the ultimate gifts is not giving up on some-one. I see Miss Hastings as one of the key characters who never gives up on Jason. Can you talk about the role Miss Hastings plays in this journey that Jason goes on?

Lee Meriwether:
Miss Hastings has been secretary to her boss, Theodore, for forty years. She adores him, respects him, and honors him, especially how he is able to bring to fruition the wishes of Red Stevens.
Miss Hastings sees the potential in Jason's character and knows he can go on this journey and follow Red's gifts to the letter. Sometimes it's a little rocky, but she still has hope, she still has faith that he will come through. It doesn't hurt that she likes the young man immediately. She also knows that the relationship between Red Stevens and her boss, Mr. Hamilton, has been one of great love over many years. All of his hopes for his companies, his holdings, all of that, rests with Jason.

Interviewer:

Is there a certain gift in the movie that resonates with you?

Lee Meriwether:

The gift of family. Were it not for that gift, so many of the other gifts would not have fallen in to place.

Interviewer:

What are your thoughts on Drew Fuller's embodiment of the character Jason?

Lee Meriwether:

Drew Fuller is a delight. He has a wonderful sense of humor. And very witty. He makes his transition into Jason's character look so easy. It's is a joy to watch.

Interviewer:

How has it been working with Bill Cobbs (played Mr. Hamilton)?

Lee Meriwether:

I am so lucky to have had this opportunity to work with Bill Cobbs. He's wonderful. I marvel at how he finds his character and then wears it like a glove. I'm blessed to be at the feet of a master, because he really has that quality of being able to become that character. It's wonderful to watch.

Interviewer:
What do you like about your character?

Lee Meriwether:
I think she's a nice woman. She cares about and is loyal to her boss. She works very hard, and was always there to help. I've tried to embody that. Hopefully, I was successful.

Interviewer:
Where do you get the inspiration for the character?

Lee Meriwether:
For most of the character, it's how I am. Or try to be. A caring individual. One who tries to understand both sides of a situation. I try to quell arguments. I'm very fortunate that in this film they dressed me with a great deal of class. If you saw me normally, you'd see jeans and T-shirts and sweatpants, things like that. But playing Miss Hastings I had to sit up straight. I personified a woman who has taken care of herself. She knows that she is the first person that anyone coming into the office of Theodore Hamilton would see.

Interview with Bill Cobbs
(played Mr. Hamilton in the movie)

Interviewer:

Tell me about your character in *The Ultimate Gift*.

Bill Cobbs:

Theodore Hamilton is a very successful lawyer. He's been Red's lawyer since they were both very young men. He has an extremely successful law firm and has handled most of Red's business for him throughout the past few decades. 'Course, Red's a billionaire, so it has been a very lucrative business for Mr. Hamilton.

Interviewer:

Tell me why you think Red gave your character a shot fresh out of law school.

Bill Cobbs:

He actually hired my character sight unseen. I think it's a very important thing to consider. We're talking maybe fifty years ago and it was rather unheard of that he would hire an African-American out of any law school, just like that, without a lot more scrutiny. So it says a lot about Red's character. Red was obviously a man who believes that your qualifications and integrity are more important than anything else.

Interviewer:
Talk about Hamilton's friendship with Red. Why did Red choose you to take Jason on this journey?

Bill Cobbs:
This is a story about a lot of things: friendship, trust, and values. So, given that, I think that we have two men who respect and admire one another for their honesty and for their work ethic. They're focused on doing the right thing. I think it's good that we have a story that takes us back to the time when people's word was their bond. You could do business on a handshake, where your ability to be trusted was very important— a time when we cared about that. I think nowadays we're led down a path that's cynical. It's refreshing to see something quite different.

Interviewer:
Talk about the dynamic between Hamilton and Jason.

Bill Cobbs:
I'm enjoying this because it's great to play a character that has ultimate power in a situation. And Hamilton's been given that power by Red, as his executor. It's also interesting to have

absolute power over a very young man who really doesn't understand some of the old fashioned values that I was talking about earlier in terms of what's important. I think it's not clichéd to say that it's better to give than to receive. A lot of people argue about that today, but I think it's still a pretty good thing. And I think this story shows why that's true. In the beginning, we see the heirs getting their little portion of this very rich man's fortune. We watch people's reactions to what they receive. And we see some very interesting reactions to people receiving large sums of money, large pieces of an estate. It really makes a comment about human nature. So my character, Attorney Hamilton, has the responsibility of taking a young man who has a lot of potential but has some very wrong ideas about life and about what's important. He gets the message in terms of the value of money, charity, kindness, loyalty, and respect.

Interviewer:
What's going on inside Hamilton? We know the objective goal, the outside goal, but what's Hamilton's attitude toward Jason when the journey first starts out?

Bill Cobbs:
When it starts out, I'm really very upset with this young man's attitude. I'm upset with his lack of a work ethic. He's really a very spoiled young man, spoiled and a very unfeeling, irresponsible person. So, I really don't expect him to do well. I have the power to put him through all kinds of tests, some of them very difficult.

And my attitude at the beginning is that he's not going to make it. I don't have to have any mercy on him. So I get a little enjoyment out of putting his feet to the fire. But there are other times when I get rather disgusted and upset that he's not getting the message. As the story progresses, we begin to see a change in Jason, and we all have a chance to look at things in a couple of different ways so we can make some evaluations for ourselves.

Interviewer:
What drew you to the story and made you want to be a part of it?

Bill Cobbs:
Everything about it. There's no profanity in it. And I get the opportunity to play a very rich man, which is fun. This is probably the most powerful character I've ever played. In a very selfish way, that's one of the things that drew me to it. And it's one that you can take your whole family to see.

Interviewer:
How do you think Drew did embodying Jason?

Bill Cobbs:
Drew is a lot like Jason in terms of the enthusiasm. Drew's a very athletic, active young man. He really enjoys his work. When you work with somebody like that, you enjoy the work, too. I think he's just perfect for the character that he's playing.

Interviewer:

What would you say is the essential message behind *The Ultimate Gift?*

Bill Cobbs:

The ultimate gift is not money. The most obvious gift in the very beginning is money. We all come to the table and everyone's assembled to see how much money, maybe how much power they're going to inherit. But the message is that material things are not what's important. We have spiritual and mental and moral things wherein our real values exists. I think the movie does a good job of reminding us about what's important.

Interviewer:

Is there a specific gift that resonates with you?

Bill Cobbs:

The gift of giving.

Interviewer:

Why is that?

Bill Cobbs:

Because in the very beginning, like everyone else, his concern is about what he's going to get. And one of the things he learns is that what he's going to give is more important ultimately.

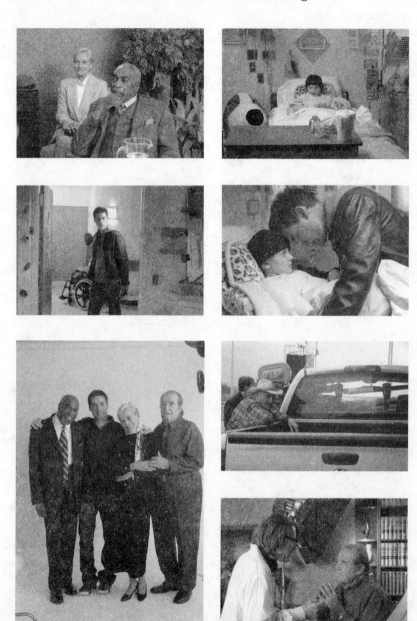